MW01628594
The Bruce-Partington Plans
3. Bentinck Street
The Final Problem
4. Bow Street
The Man with the Twisted Lip
5. Brook Street
The Resident Patient
6. Cannon Street Station
The Man with the Twisted Lip
7. Carlton House Terrace
The Priory School
8. Charing Cross Station
The Abbey Grange
9. Church Street
The Six Napoleons
10. Conduit Street
The Empty House
11. Covent Garden Market
The Blue Carbuncle
12. Downing Street
The Naval Treaty
13. Euston Station
The Priory School
14. Farringdon Street
The Red-Headed League
15. High Holborn
Wisteria Lodge
16. Liverpool Street Station
The Dancing Men
17. London Bridge
The Sign of Four
20. Park Lane
The Empty House
21. Russell Square
The Dancing Men
22. St. Paul's
The Sign of Four
23. Saffron Hill
The Six Napoleons
24. Scotland Yard
25. Shaftesbury Avenue
The Greek Interpreter
26. Stock Exchange
The Bruce-Partington Plans
27. The Strand
A Study in Scarlet
28. The Temple
A Scandal in Bohemia
29. Tower of London
The Sign of Four
30. Trafalgar Square
The Hound of the Baskervilles
31. Victoria Station
Silver Blaze
32. Vincent Square
The Sign of Four
33. Waterloo Station
The Crooked Man
34. Westminster Pier
The Sign of Four

GRANADA COMPANION
Number One: *A Sherlock Holmes Album*

Text by Kenneth Harris

Edited by Michael Cox and Andrew Robinson
Picture Research by Bill Hill and Vanessa Lees
All TV production pictures copyright Granada Television and used with their permission
Production co-ordinated by Bill Hill

Design by Alan Pinnock
Published by Karizzma
Typeset by Tangram (London) Ltd
Printed in England by Julian Bloom Printing Ltd
Printing House
Carpenters Road
London E15

ISBN 0-9513000-0-8

In the United States of America the Granada films are seen in the PBS series *MYSTERY!* originated by WGBH Boston and made possible by a grant from the Mobil Corporation.

1887 ❋ 1987

Introduction by VINCENT PRICE

I HAVE lived two lives. By profession I am an actor. In my later years I have specialised in films of horror, mystery and detection. I have loved every minute of it. By vocation I am an art historian. I began my studies fifty years ago in the University of London at the Courtauld Institute. I have loved every minute of that life too. My two lives, my two loves, harmonise when I watch Granada Television's classic series, *The Adventures of Sherlock Holmes.*

Sherlock Holmes, said that master of mystery and suspense, Orson Welles, 'is a gentleman who never lived – and who will never die.' Immortality set in a century ago. Never has the great detective been so faithfully and dramatically portrayed as he has in this series. But to reproduce the personality and the methods of the unique Holmes is not enough: to get the best of him he must be presented against the fascinating background of his Victorian times. Holmes performed his breath-taking feats of deduction in the period of Britain's greatest power and influence, the reign of Queen Victoria. The series shows us the mind and methods of Sherlock Holmes against an authentic and artistic reconstruction of the human setting in which he was a living part.

Speaking as a professional in the field of horror, mystery and detection, and also as a student of the history of art, I say this: each episode which has been seen so far – and I have seen those which are to come – is gripping, exciting, and at times horrific. But it is also elegant, historical and well researched.

I think Arthur Conan Doyle, the creator of Sherlock Holmes, but also a historian, artist, writer, and uncompromising critic, a man very hard to please, would have rejoiced in the achievement. Even Sherlock Holmes, the most fastidious of men, would have approved, and, being something of a prima donna who felt never properly appreciated, would have granted that this time posterity had got him right.

The great advantage of Victorian times for us is that they are near enough to our own for those who have the skill to study and reproduce them to make them come alive. Yet the period is far enough back in time to excite our romantic interest in the past. It offers us both worlds, the near and the far. In our own generation we have the extra advantage of being able to see them on television, the medium which can bring the scenes and sights and sounds of those times to our eyes and ears as books, radio and even the cinema were never able to. The colour and drama of Victorian times is great stuff for the television camera. I speak as one who began his acting career as Prince Albert in *Victoria Regina*, and ever after retained great interest in the period.

But in art as in life it is the human element that counts. Unless the characters come over strong, clear and real, the film or television programme, the book or the painting, will fall short of what was possible, and, indeed, may fail.

Inevitably all productions stand or fall by the casting and playing of Sherlock Holmes. I do not envy the producer who has to choose his Holmes, or the actor who decides to play the part. Nearly a century of stage, then film, then radio, then television, has begotten a succession of Sherlock Holmeses, many of the highest class. The competition has been enormous in quality and quantity. There have been some failures; there have been some great successes. Michael Cox's choice of Jeremy Brett to play Holmes in this series was inspired. Mr Brett brings just that degree of novelty and differentness to his portrayal of Holmes – but not too much – to give the character yet another incandescent lease of life. Nearly fifty years ago, Basil Rathbone did the same. I rate Mr Brett with Basil Rathbone as the two most convincing and exciting Sherlock Holmes I have ever seen.

The text and illustrations of this album are centred upon Sherlock Holmes and the television series of which he is the star. Without the new series there would have been no album, but nevertheless, the publication stands in its own right, both as a contribution to what we know of Holmes, of his creator Conan Doyle, and of the times in which he lived, and also, as a delightful and expertly chosen presentation of Victoriana the setting of the great detective's feats. The very cover of this publication is the message: eyes will always be focused on Sherlock Holmes, but he is best observed in that late Victorian England in which he first made his name.

Vincent Price

CONAN DOYLE

by Kenneth Harris

O SOONER had Conan Doyle made Sherlock Holmes the most popular character in fiction since Robin Hood than he made up his mind to kill him.

What was the reason for this curious decision? It was that Conan Doyle did not want to go down in history as a crime writer but as the author of historical novels. It irked him that though the public admired *The White Company*, *Sir Nigel* and *Micah Clarke* as much as the works of Sir Walter Scott, they liked the Sherlock Holmes stories more.

So, writing to his mother about the twelfth and last Sherlock Holmes story he intended to produce, Conan Doyle recorded: 'I think of slaying Holmes...and winding him up for good and for all.' His mother, a formidable lady whom he always called 'The Ma'am', wrote back in fury: 'You won't! You can't! You *musn't!*'

He didn't, not that time; but two years later he did. In *The Final Problem* Holmes wrestles on the edge of a precipice with the Napoleon of crime, Professor Moriarty, and the two of them, according to the story, hurtle hundreds of feet to their death at the bottom of the Reichenbach Falls.

Half England was heart-broken; the other half was outraged. 'Bring him back, please' wrote tens of thousands of readers to the *Strand Magazine*, in which the story had been printed. Twenty thousand of them cancelled their subscriptions. 'You fiend, you murderer', one woman shouted at Conan Doyle in the street. Young city men went to their offices with black bands around their hats. No mourning like it was seen until Queen Victoria died seven years later.

For ten years Conan Doyle was impervious to tears, threats and lucrative contracts. When the American actor, William Gillette, constructed a play about Holmes, and cabled, 'MAY I MARRY HOLMES?' Conan Doyle cabled back: 'MARRY HIM OR MURDER HIM OR DO WHAT YOU LIKE WITH HIM.'

Ten years after Holmes had 'died' the *Strand* made Conan Doyle an offer he could not refuse. Holmes reappeared. London gave a great cheer. People queued outside the *Strand* offices in case the first Holmes issue was sold out in the shops. It was. The young city men went to work with orchids in their button-holes.

In 1902 Conan Doyle was knighted, reportedly for having written pamphlets defending the Government's policies in the Boer War. The buzz was that he was knighted because he had promised the King to bring Holmes back. Sir Arthur girded himself and wrote another thirty-four stories over the next twenty-five years, but never became reconciled to his creation's success.

This may seem extraordinary. But Conan Doyle was an extraordinary man, not only in the sense of being out of the ordinary, which he certainly was, but in the sense of being difficult to understand. There were strange contradictions in his character.

That he was out of the ordinary stands out a mile. He was an erect six feet two, built like a bull, as strong as an ox, with a grip like a grizzly bear. He was also a top rate amateur boxer, a first class cricketer, an outstanding soccer player, and a fearless horseman.

His stamina and powers of concentration were almost superhuman. He could work from morning to night for several days locked in his study, trays of food piling up uneaten outside his door, managing with a few hours sleep. He could write fiction or fact, political pamphlet, newspaper article or book, as fast as any man who had ever lived.

His versatility was incredible. His stories of horror and mystery rival those of Edgar Allan Poe. His novels about weird worlds which never existed are on a par with those of H.G.Wells, *The Lost World*, for example. Nothing in the genre excels his comic stories about Brigadier Gerard, a swashbuckling hussar in Napoleon's army. He wrote histories of the Boer War and of the first World War. He was a pioneer of science-fiction.

Unlike many distinguished writers he also had a celebrated and influential career in public life. He stood twice for Parliament, and championed many public causes, often incurring financial loss and hostile criticism.

Drawing on powers of detection and deduction not inferior to those of Sherlock Holmes, he solved many cases brought to him by anguished citizens, and on more than one occasion corrected the course of British justice, notably by setting in train the events which led to the quashing of Oscar Slater's murder sentence and the payment of compensation.

All these remarkable achievements apart, however, Conan Doyle was extraordinary in the other sense – of being a strange man, a man of many contradictions.

Born in 1859, brought up a firm Roman Catholic, as a young man he renounced his faith in the name of reason. Yet he soon became very interested in communication with the dead, and for the last fifteen years of his life was a convert to the least credible of religions: Spiritualism.

For years he attended seances and talked with mediums whom Holmes, and even dear old Watson, would have seen through in a flash. Yet he continued to credit what most people dismiss as rubbish until he died, in 1930, aged 71, his loyalty to his new faith having cost him the peerage which King George V wished him to have.

There was another contradiction in his make-up: though fascinated by the critical intellect, his true love was romance. Sherlock Holmes was modelled on Professor Joseph Bell, who taught medicine at Edinburgh when Conan Doyle was a student there. Bell deduced things about people just by looking at them. 'This man is a left-handed cobbler. You'll obsairve, gentlemen, the worn places on the corduroy breeks where a cobbler rests his lapstone? The right-hand side, you'll note, is far more worn than the left...' The first collection of Holmes stories was dedicated to Bell, 'my old Teacher.'

Yet, Conan Doyle's heart was not with the

Professor Bells of this world, but with the knights and ladies of the age of chivalry (which Holmes, and even Watson, could have told him never existed).

Romance not reason was what made Conan Doyle tick. His head was magnificent, but it was ruled by his heart. His ideal was the wandering knight in shining armour saving the ethereally clad maiden from some fate worse than death, not a hard-headed hawk-eyed sleuth armed with a magnifying glass and a wad of litmus paper.

There were two sides to Conan Doyle, and they were barely reconcilable. Consequently, though he enjoyed much of his life, he was not consistently happy. He suffered from depressions. He could be irritable, aggressive, and sometimes subject to outbursts of temper.

Circumstances could account for much of this. He married Louise Hawkins when they were both very young, and though he was extremely fond of her he was never in love. Her health was poor – she died before she was fifty – and the marriage was not a fulfilment for him. For the last nine years of it he had been deeply in love with a charming and talented young woman, Jean Leckie, fourteen years younger than he was. By all accounts he remained puritanically – chivalrously? – faithful to his wife. He married Jean Leckie a year after Louise's death.

During the previous nine years, nurse to his wife and celibate to Jean, he must have lived under great stress. Escape may have meant more to him than reality, chivalry more than crime detection, the past more than the present.

By any standard, Conan Doyle is a study in contradictions. Here is a man who after his experiences in the front lines of the Boer War pressed the War Office to clothe the infantry in khaki instead of red coats and to replace the cavalry with tanks and rifles: realism versus romanticism. He foresaw the coming of the first world war and the crucial role of the submarine. He owned motor-cycles and motor cars when most people thought these would remain toys. He urged the Swiss to import skis from Norway and create a new national sports industry.

Yet the make-believe past which never existed

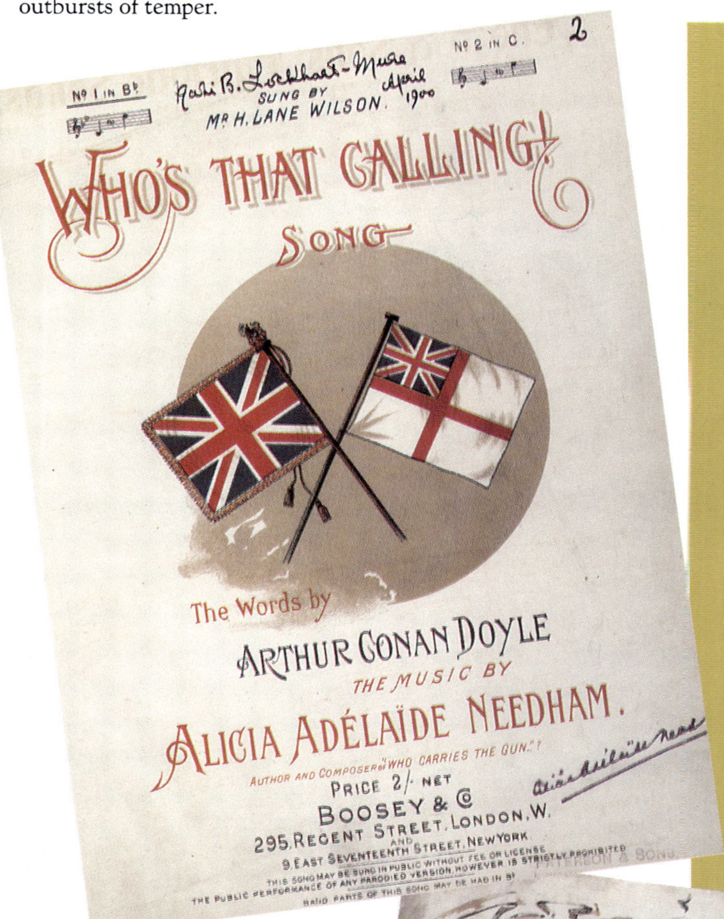

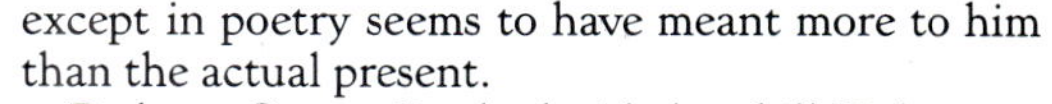

except in poetry seems to have meant more to him than the actual present.

Perhaps Conan Doyle decided to kill Holmes so soon after he had created him not so much because the stories diverted public attention from the historical novels, but because he recognised in Holmes the number one enemy of the world he would have preferred to live in. 'He takes my mind off better things', he told his mother. Conan Doyle wanted to inhabit the world of the knight errant, of chivalry, purity, of spirits and a roseate hereafter. Holmes would have scoffed at this.

When Watson, describing an old house, gets as far as 'a high sun-baked wall mottled with lichens and topped with moss', Holmes interrupts with 'Cut out the poetry, Watson. I note that it has a high brick wall'. Conan Doyle would never have spoken like that to Watson. 'What a brute you are Holmes!' he must have thought as he recorded those callous words, perhaps snarling to himself as he did so, even more venomously than Moriarty would have: 'Holmes will have to go'.

So a contract went out on Holmes. Fortunately for him – and for us – a contract of another kind came in, and it was large enough to bring the great detective back to a life which has never since been threatened.

OPPOSITE
The Strand Magazine, August 1896.

ABOVE
Queen Victoria in her robes of state. From the painting by F. Winterhalter.

* * * * *

Conan Doyle not only supported the Boer War but wrote a patriotic song about it.

THE STORIES AND THE CASTS

A SCANDAL IN BOHEMIA

*

NOT previously interested in the female sex, Sherlock Holmes informs Watson that he has encountered '*the* woman': Irene Adler. Will she ruin the King of Bohemia, about to be married, by revealing information about his previous love life? Holmes has only three days to retrieve the compromising evidence. Will he make it?

Dramatised by	Alexander Baron
Sherlock Holmes	Jeremy Brett
Doctor Watson	David Burke
Irene Adler	Gayle Hunnicutt
King of Bohemia	Wolf Kahler
Godfrey Norton	Michael Carter
Mrs Hudson	Rosalie Williams
John	Max Faulkner
Mrs Willard	Tessa Worsley
Clergyman	Will Tacey
Cabby	Tim Pearce
Director	Paul Annett

The Dancing Men
Then, as now, a London policeman was a reliable guide

THE DANCING MEN

*

THE young wife of a Norfolk squire is obviously terrified by matchstick men chalked on a garden seat, but tries to hide her fear. More matchstick men appear, so her husband consults Holmes, who sees that the dancing men are a code, which he succeeds in cracking, but not before there has been tragedy and death.

Dramatised by	Anthony Skene
Sherlock Holmes	Jeremy Brett
Doctor Watson	David Burke
Hilton Cubitt	Tenniel Evans
Elsie Cubitt	Betsy Brantley
Abe Slaney	Eugene Lipinski
Saunders	Wendy Jane Walker
Mrs King	Lorraine Peters
Inspector Martin	David Ross
Walker	Paul Jaynes
Doctor Carthew	Bernard Atha
Director	John Bruce

A Scandal in Bohemia
'To Sherlock Holmes she is always the woman'

The Dancing Men
Back to the blackboard to break a devilish code

The Dancing Men
Leighton Hall near Carnforth used as *Ridling Thorpe Manor*, Norfolk

THE NAVAL TREATY

*

COPYING a highly secret treaty late at night in the Foreign Office, a young diplomat leaves his desk for a few seconds and returns to find that the document has disappeared. How could anybody have located and removed the missive in so short a time? His career faces ruin, but, much more important, publication of the treaty would precipitate an international crisis. Holmes rescues career and country.

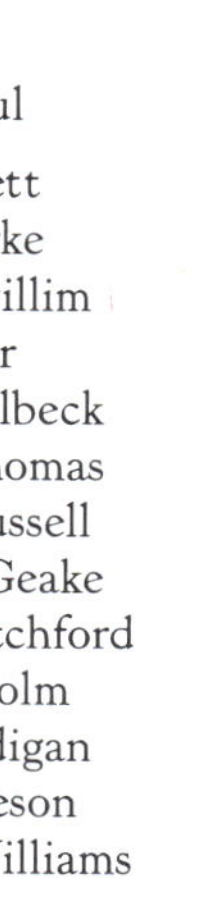

Dramatised by	Jeremy Paul
Sherlock Holmes	Jeremy Brett
Doctor Watson	David Burke
Percy Phelps	David Gwillim
Doctor Ferrier	John Taylor
Annie Harrison	Alison Skilbeck
Joseph Harrison	Gareth Thomas
Lord Holdhurst	Ronald Russell
Charles Gorot	Nicholas Geake
Mrs Tangey	Pamela Pitchford
Tangey	John Malcolm
Inspector Forbes	David Rodigan
Miss Tangey	Eve Matheson
Mrs Hudson	Rosalie Williams
Director	Alan Grint

The Solitary Cyclist
'My employer, Mr Carruthers, takes a great deal of interest in me...a girl always knows'

THE SOLITARY CYCLIST

*

AN attractive girl cycles six miles along a lonely road once a week to visit her mother. Whenever she comes to a certain stretch a bearded stranger begins to follow her at a distance. If she slows, he slows; if she stops, he stops. At a certain point he disappears. Among other coups Holmes saves the maiden from a fate worse than death.

Dramatised by	Alan Plater
Sherlock Holmes	Jeremy Brett
Doctor Watson	David Burke
Violet Smith	Barbara Wilshere
Carruthers	John Castle
Woodley	Michael Siberry
Williamson	Ellis Dale
Sarah Carruthers	Sarah Aitchison
Landlord	Stafford Gordon
Peter	Simon Bleackley
Mrs Hudson	Rosalie Williams
Mrs Dixon	Penny Gowling
Director	Paul Annett

The Solitary Cyclist
Willington Hall as *Chiltern Grange*

The Naval Treaty
'What a lovely thing a rose is'

The Solitary Cyclist
Violet Smith on her weekly bicycle ride to Farnham Station

THE CROOKED MAN

*

AFTER hearing a frightful quarrel in the morning room, the servants find the Colonel lying dead from a gash in the back of his head, his face a mask of horror, and his wife stretched unconscious on the sofa. Holmes deduces that a third person was in that room, and discovers the traces of a mysterious animal. All is made clear.

Dramatised by	Alfred Shaughnessy
Sherlock Holmes	Jeremy Brett
Doctor Watson	David Burke
Henry Wood	Norman Jones
Young Henry Wood	Michael Lumsden
Col James Barclay	Denys Hawthorne
Young James Barclay	James Wilby
Nancy Barclay	Lisa Daniely
Young Nancy Barclay	Catherine Rabett
Major Murphy	Paul Chapman
Miss Morrison	Fiona Shaw
Jane	Shelagh Stephenson
Bates	Colin Campbell
Mrs Fenning	Maggie Holland
Director	Alan Grint

The Crooked Man
'You see me now with my back like a camel and my ribs all awry, but there was a time when Corporal Henry Wood was the smartest man in the 117th Foot'

THE SPECKLED BAND

✻

BEAUTIFUL, in love and engaged to be married, Helen Stoner fears for her life in her tyrannical step-father's remote country house, where her sister died mysteriously screaming 'the Speckled Band!'. Holmes and Watson visit the house in secret, and after a creepy night, and a terrible death, put Miss Stoner's fears to rest.

Dramatised by	Jeremy Paul
Sherlock Holmes	Jeremy Brett
Doctor Watson	David Burke
Doctor Grimesby Roylott	Jeremy Kemp
Helen Stoner	Rosalyn Landor
Julia Stoner	Denise Armon
Driver	John Gill
Mrs Hudson	Rosalie Williams
Thorne	Timothy Condren
Percy Armitage	Stephen Mallatratt
Director	John Bruce

The Speckled Band
Helen Stoner who lived in fear that her sister's tragic fate would be repeated in her own case

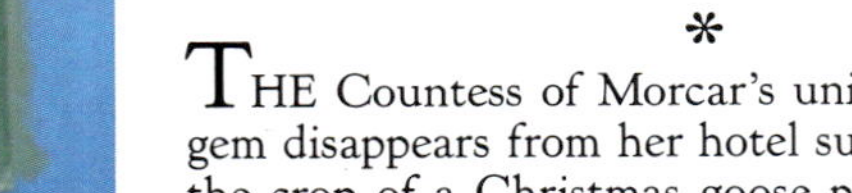

THE BLUE CARBUNCLE

✻

THE Countess of Morcar's unique and priceless gem disappears from her hotel suite to reappear in the crop of a Christmas goose paid for in weekly instalments by an impoverished man of letters. Holmes's powers of deduction are seen at their best before the criminal's goose is cooked.

Dramatised by	Paul Finney
Sherlock Holmes	Jeremy Brett
Doctor Watson	David Burke
Inspector Bradstreet	Brian Miller
Mrs Hudson	Rosalie Williams
The Countess of Morcar	Rosalind Knight
John Horner	Desmond McNamara
James Ryder	Ken Campbell
Catherine Cusack	Ros Simmons
Henry Baker	Frank Middlemass
Windigate	Don McCorkindale
Jennie Horner	Amelda Brown
Peterson	Frank Mills
Breckenridge	Eric Allan
Mrs Oakshott	Maggie Jones
Director	David Carson

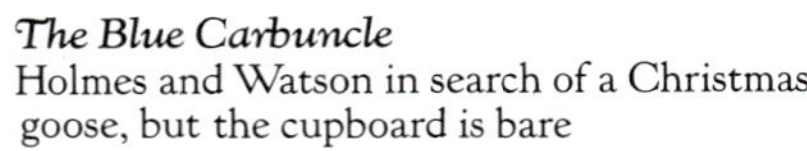

The Blue Carbuncle
Holmes and Watson in search of a Christmas goose, but the cupboard is bare

THE COPPER BEECHES

✻

A young governess at a remote house in Hampshire agrees, because she is so highly paid, to cut short her chestnut hair, wear a blue dress and sit frequently with her back to the drawing-room window. She realizes she is being observed from the road by a man, whom her employer soon asks her to wave away. Alarming things now happen in the house. Holmes arrives in the nick of time.

Dramatised by	Bill Craig
Sherlock Holmes	Jeremy Brett
Doctor Watson	David Burke
Violet Hunter	Natasha Richardson
Jephro Rucastle	Joss Ackland
Mrs Rucastle	Lottie Ward
Edward Rucastle	Stuart Shinberg
Fowler	Michael Loney
Toller	Peter Jonfield
Mrs Toller	Angela Browne
Miss Stoper	Patience Collier
Alice	Rachel Ambler
Director	Paul Annett

The Copper Beeches
Violet Hunter whose salary was trebled because she cut her hair and wore this dress

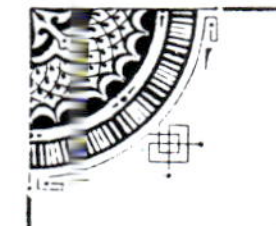

THE GREEK INTERPRETER

✻

MELAS, a Greek interpreter, is taken by night in a carriage with covered windows to a house where he is made to interpret for a man who is being kept prisoner, and is bravely refusing to sign a document. A beautiful woman bursts upon the scene. Melas is hustled off, and is dumped at a distant roadside. Holmes hears his grim story, and goes into action.

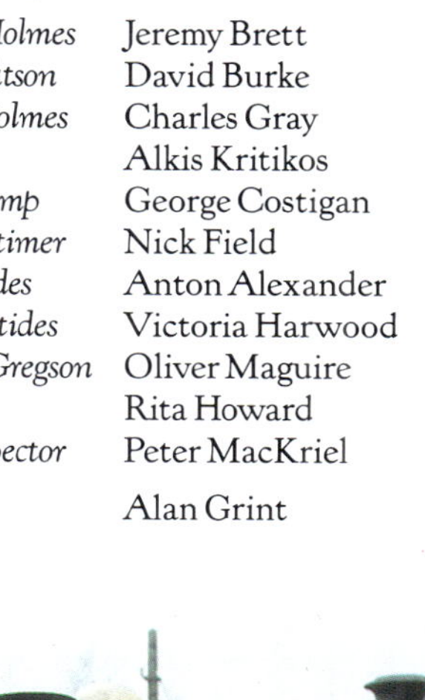

Dramatised by	Derek Marlowe
Sherlock Holmes	Jeremy Brett
Doctor Watson	David Burke
Mycroft Holmes	Charles Gray
Mr Melas	Alkis Kritikos
Wilson Kemp	George Costigan
Harold Latimer	Nick Field
Paul Kratides	Anton Alexander
Sophy Kratides	Victoria Harwood
Inspector Gregson	Oliver Maguire
Mrs Stern	Rita Howard
Ticket Inspector	Peter MacKriel
Director	Alan Grint

The Greek Interpreter
'...his brother possessed even keener faculties than he did himself'

The Greek Interpreter
'Mycroft has his rails and he runs on them'

THE NORWOOD BUILDER

✻

JOHN Hector McFarlane rushes to Holmes: he is about to be arrested for murder. Jonas Oldacre, a Norwood builder, has disappeared, and McFarlane's stick, blood-stained, has been found in his house. The police are convinced that McFarlane is guilty, but Holmes dramatically produces a new witness, and a spectacular dénouement.

Dramatised by	Richard Harris
Sherlock Holmes	Jeremy Brett
Doctor Watson	David Burke
Mrs Lexington	Rosalie Crutchley
Lestrade	Colin Jeavons
John Hector McFarlane	Matthew Solon
Jonas Oldacre	Jonathan Adams
Mrs McFarlane	Helen Ryan
Mrs Hudson	Rosalie Williams
Constable	Andy Rashleigh
Tramp	Anthony Langdon
Seafaring Tramp	Ted Carroll
Director	Ken Grieve

The Norwood Builder
'Mr Holmes...I could go to gaol happy if I knew that you were working for me outside'

The Resident Patient
'I would never trust a banker, Mr Holmes...what little I have is in that box'

THE RESIDENT PATIENT

✻

A Mr Blessington, having heard of young Mr Trevelyan's brilliance as a medical student, sets him up in practice in Brook Street, as an investment, taking a share of the profits, and moving in as a resident patient. The premises are subsequently visited by other patients, news of whom so much terrifies Mr Blessington that he begs Mr Trevelyan to consult Sherlock Holmes.

Dramatised by	Derek Marlowe
Sherlock Holmes	Jeremy Brett
Doctor Watson	David Burke
Blessington	Patrick Newell
Doctor Percy Trevelyan	Nicholas Clay
Mrs Hudson	Rosalie Williams
Father (Biddle)	Tim Barlow
Son (Hayward)	Brett Forrest
Cartwright	Charles Cork
Inspector Lanner	John Ringham
Nora	Lucy Ann Wilson
Detective	Norman Mills
Carpenter	Dusty Young
Director	David Carson

THE RED-HEADED LEAGUE

*

A conspicuously red-headed pawnbroker is advised to apply for admission to the Red-Headed League, which he successfully does, being paid extremely well by them to perform easy part-time duties. One day he comes to work and finds his employers have departed without trace. Holmes foresees and prevents a great crime, and catches the criminals if not red-headed all red-handed.

Dramatised by	John Hawkesworth
Sherlock Holmes	Jeremy Brett
Doctor Watson	David Burke
Mr Merryweather	John Woodnutt
Moriarty	Eric Porter
Jabez Wilson	Roger Hammond
Vincent Spaulding (Clay)	Tim McInnerny
Doorman	Reginald Stewart
Duncan Ross	Richard Wilson
Accountant	Ian Bleasdale
Peter Jones	John Labanowski
Policeman	Harry Goodier
Director	John Bruce

The Final Problem
'It would be a great pleasure if you could come on to the Continent with me'

THE FINAL PROBLEM

*

THE infamous Professor Moriarty's diabolical schemes are so much frustrated by Sherlock Holmes that he resolves to liquidate him. Holmes accepts that the world is too small to hold them both, and the good and evil geniuses meet on the edge of the precipitous Reichenbach Falls in Switzerland for a wrestling match from which only one or none will return alive.

Dramatised by	John Hawkesworth
Sherlock Holmes	Jeremy Brett
Doctor Watson	David Burke
Professor Moriarty	Eric Porter
Mrs Hudson	Rosalie Williams
Director of the Louvre	Olivier Pierre
Minister of the Interior	Claude Lé Saché
Artist	Michael Goldie
Young Expert	Paul Sirr
American Millionaire	Robert Henderson
Porter	Jim Dunk
Steiler	Paul Humpoletz
Swiss Youth	Simon Adams
Director	Alan Grint

The Red-Headed League
'I wish to the Lord, Mr Wilson, that I was a red-headed man'

The Final Problem
A lesson in forgery – with a famous example

THE EMPTY HOUSE

*

HOLMES did not, after all, plunge to his death in the Reichenbach Falls. Moriarty did. Why then does Holmes, accompanied by Watson, stealthily return to Baker Street at night by a roundabout route through the back alleys of the neighbourhood? And what has this to do with the mysterious murder of the Hon Ronald Adair?

Dramatised by	John Hawkesworth
Sherlock Holmes	Jeremy Brett
Doctor Watson	Edward Hardwicke
Mrs Hudson	Rosalie Williams
Colonel Sebastian Moran	Patrick Allen
Inspector Lestrade	Colin Jeavons
The Hon Ronald Adair	Paul Lacoux
Coroner	James Bree
Mr Murray	Robert Addie
Sir John Hardy	Richard Bebb
The Countess of Maynooth	Naomi Buch
Director	Howard Baker

The Empty House
'I realised more clearly than I had ever done the loss which the community had sustained by the death of Sherlock Holmes'.

THE ABBEY GRANGE

*

SIR EUSTACE Brackenstall, drunken brute, is found clubbed to death, the evidence of his beautiful long-suffering wife, whom he had recently beaten up, convincing the police that burglars are to blame. Holmes studies three wineglasses, a blood-stained poker, a broken bell-rope, the frozen pond in the park, and unmasks the real murderer.

Dramatised by	T R Bowen
Sherlock Holmes	Jeremy Brett
Doctor Watson	Edward Hardwicke
Inspector Hopkins	Paul Williamson
Sir Eustace Brackenstall	Conrad Phillips
Lady Mary Brackenstall	Anne Louise Lambert
Theresa Wright	Zulema Dene
Captain Crocker	Oliver Tobias
Mr. Viviani	Nicolas Chagrin
Director	Peter Hammond

The Abbey Grange
'I am the wife of Sir Eustace Brackenstall'.

The Empty House
'I am glad to stretch myself, Watson. It is no joke when a tall man has to take a foot off his stature for several hours'.

The Abbey Grange
'I hope that you have not come to cross-examine me again'.

THE SECOND STAIN

*

'THEN, SIR, prepare for war', says Holmes when the Prime Minister asks him to recover the unspeakably secret document which has been removed from the Foreign Secretary's despatch box even though he has not parted with the one and only key. Was there a war? Anyway, you'd never guess who got at that despatch box.

Dramatised by	John Hawkesworth
Sherlock Holmes	Jeremy Brett
Doctor Watson	Edward Hardwicke
Lady Hilda Trelawney Hope	Patricia Hodge
The Rt. Hon. Trelawney Hope	Stuart Wilson
Lord Bellinger	Harry Andrews
Lestrade	Colin Jeavons
Bates	Alan Bennion
Madame Henri Fournaye	Yvonne Orengo
Mrs Hudson	Rosalie Williams
MacPherson	Sean Scanlan
Eduardo Lucas	Yves Beneyton
Director	John Bruce

The Second Stain
'You think, sir, that unless this document is recovered there will be war?
'I think it very probable'.

The Second Stain
The cheek was lovely but it was paled with emotion; the eyes were bright but it was the brightness of fever; the sensitive mouth was tight and drawn in an effort after self-command. Terror – not beauty – was what sprang first to the eye.

The Second Stain
'There is a second stain but it does not correspond with the other; see for yourself'.

The Musgrave Ritual
'The Butler of Hurlstone is always a thing that is remembered by all who visit us'.

THE MUSGRAVE RITUAL

*

WORTHY of comparison with Edgar Allan Poe's *The Gold Bug*. Holmes displays his knowledge of trigonometry, cracks a two-hundred-and-fifty-year-old code, reveals what the missing butler saw and where he is to be found. He also discovers an object of the greatest historical importance.

Dramatised by	Jeremy Paul
Sherlock Holmes	Jeremy Brett
Doctor Watson	Edward Hardwicke
Reginald Musgrave	Michael Culver
Richard Brunton	James Hazeldine
Rachel Howells	Johanna Kirby
Janet Tregallis	Teresa Banham
Inspector Fereday	Ian Marter
Tregallis	Patrick Blackwell
Director	David Carson

The Musgrave Ritual
A splendid park, with fine old timber, surrounded the house, and the lake lay close to the avenue about two hundred yards away from the building.

The Man with the Twisted Lip
'Holmes! What on earth are you doing in this den?'

THE MAN WITH THE TWISTED LIP

*

THE wealthy Neville St Clair disappears, last seen, unaccountably, at the window of a room in the vilest opium den in London's dockland. Boone, a hideous beggar, occupant of the room, is charged with murdering St Clair, and throwing the body into the river. Holmes gets the real culprit to come clean.

Dramatised by	Alan Plater
Sherlock Holmes	Jeremy Brett
Doctor Watson	Edward Hardwicke
Mrs Hudson	Rosalie Williams
Neville St Clair/Hugh Boone	Clive Francis
Mrs St Clair	Eleanor David
Isa Whitney	Terence Longdon
Mrs Whitney	Patricia Garwood
Inspector Bradstreet	Denis Lill
Lascar	Albert Moses
Constables	Dudley James Robin Marchal
Director	Patrick Lau

THE PRIORY SCHOOL

*

THE Headmaster of the exclusive Priory School rushes to Baker Street, faints on Holmes's hearth rug, and, revived by Watson's brandy, begs Holmes to recover the Duke of Holdernesse's nine-year-old son who has disappeared from his dormitory in the dead of night. High drama, murder and mystery on the eerie Derbyshire moors.

Dramatised by	T R Bowen
Sherlock Holmes	Jeremy Brett
Doctor Watson	Edward Hardwicke
Doctor Huxtable	Christopher Benjamin
Mr Aveling	Michael Bertenshaw
James Wilder	Nicholas Gecks
Duke of Holdernesse	Alan Howard
Rivers	William Abney
Reuben Hayes	Jack Carr
Mrs Hayes	Brender Elder
Mrs Hudson	Rosalie Williams
Lord Arthur Saltire	Nissar Moti
Caunter	Mark Turin
Director	John Madden

THE SIX NAPOLEONS

*

SOMEBODY is going around London smashing busts of Napoleon. Murder is involved. Is an anti-Napoleon nut at large? Or is there a more sinister explanation? The police are baffled. Holmes detects a pattern in these happenings and finally busts the criminal.

Dramatised by	John Kane
Sherlock Holmes	Jeremy Brett
Doctor Watson	Edward Hardwicke
Harker	Eric Sykes
Lucretia	Marina Sirtis
Venucci	Steve Plytas
Beppo	Emile Wolk
Morse Hudson	Gerald Campion
Beppo's Cousin	Nadio Fortune
Mr Sandeford	Jeffrey Gardiner
Mr Brown	Michael Logan
Pietro	Vincenzo Nicoli
Mandelstam	Vernon Dobtcheff
Director	David Carson

The Six Napoleons
He was introduced to us as the owner of the house; Mr Horace Harker.

The Six Napoleons
'Yes, sir, it was I who sold Dr. Barnicot his two statues. Disgraceful, sir! A Nihilist plot, that's what I make it'.

The Man with the Twisted Lip
Mrs St. Clair...did some shopping, proceeded to the Company's office, got her packet, and found herself exactly at 4.35 walking through Swandam Lane.

The Priory School
The Priory is without exception the best and most select preparatory school in England.

The Sign of Four
Outside the Lyceum theatre: *'Are you the parties that come with Miss Morstan?'*

The Sign of Four
'Well, sir, you have been very fair-spoken to me, though I can see that I have you to thank that I have these bracelets upon my wrist'.

THE SIGN OF FOUR

Dramatised by	John Hawkesworth
Sherlock Holmes	Jeremy Brett
Doctor Watson	Edward Hardwicke
Small	John Thaw
Mary Morstan	Jenny Seagrove
Thaddeus Sholto	Ronald Lacey
Athelney Jones	Emrys James
Tonga	Kiran Shah
Wiggins	Courtenay Roper-Knight
Lal Chowder	Ishak Bux
Mr Smith	Dave Atkins
McMurdo	Alf Joint
Major Sholto	Robin Hunter
Mrs Smith	Lila Kaye
Khartar Singh	Badi Uzzaman
Sherman	Gordon Gostelow
Captain Morstan	Terence Skelton
Williams	Derek Deadman
Inderjit Singh	Ravinder Singh Reyatt
Achmet	Renu Setna
Director	Peter Hammond

The Sign of Four
'There is something devilish in this, Watson. What do you make of it?'

The Sign of Four
With lolling tongue and blinking eyes Toby stood upon the cask, looking from one to the other of us for some sign of appreciation.

PRODUCTION

The Adventures were produced by MICHAEL COX
The Return and *The Sign of Four* by JUNE WYNDHAM DAVIES
Design by MICHAEL GRIMES, TIM WILDING and MARGARET COOMBES
Costume Design by ESTHER DEAN
Make-up by GLENDA WOOD and SUE MILTON
Music by PATRICK GOWERS
Executive Producer Michael Cox

Playing Sherlock Holmes: A Profile of JEREMY BRETT

ORE THAN a hundred actors have played the role of Sherlock Holmes, universally the best known detective created in English crime fiction, on stage, screen or television. The roll of honour includes such famous names as William Gillette, Arthur Wontner, Clive Brook, Basil Rathbone, Peter Cushing and Christopher Lee.

Vincent Price says in the foreword to this book that the two best Holmeses he has ever seen, and he has been seeing portrayals of Holmes for more than fifty years, are Basil Rathbone and Jeremy Brett.

One of the most attractive things about Mr Brett is that though he enjoys his success he seems still to be surprised by it.

'When Michael Cox, the executive producer of the series, asked me in 1982 if I would play Holmes, I was very hesitant.

'First, there were all the Holmeses who had gone before. What could I add? Indeed, could I survive in such competition?

'I had aspired to be a Shakespearian actor, serving my apprenticeship under the wing of Lord Olivier at the National Theatre. If there is anything about my acting which can be commended I owe it to him. But could what I had learned from Olivier be applied to the portrayal of Sherlock Holmes on television?

'How could I follow Basil Rathbone? Conan Doyle told the great American actor, Gillette, "You *are* Holmes." If I had ever had the honour of meeting Rathbone – I've met some of his friends, and his godson, and they say he was a splendid person – I'd have said the same: "You *are* Sherlock Holmes."

'I'm *not*. I don't even *look* like Holmes. Rathbone hardly needed make-up. He could almost walk straight on to the set. It takes Susan Milton at least forty-five minutes to put my make-up on.

'And I'm not like Holmes as a person. He was a tremendous realist; I'm a romantic. He was an introvert; I'm an extrovert. He was immensely serious; I'm rather a jolly chap.

'Anyway, Mike Cox seemed keen for me to play the role, and he impressed me at once as a man of excellent judgement. That was one inducement for me to have a go.

'The other was that he was also very keen for Granada to screen a series of Sherlock Holmes stories which got the Conan Doyle text absolutely correct. In particular Mike wanted to get the first faithful rendering of Watson, and of the relationship between him and Holmes.

'He got it. The first Watson I was cast with, David Burke, was the breakthrough for the "real" Watson. The second, Edward Hardwicke, followed up with equal integrity and sensitivity.

'Watson had been hammed up in many film and television productions, and had often been made to look an ass. I think Mike Cox has prevented that ever happening again.

'It's difficult for me to say what I may have given to the image of Holmes. Faith to Conan Doyle's text, certainly. I've worked very hard at that, encouraged by Mike Cox, and by Peter Hammond, the director. I carry my annotated volume around with me.

'Also, I've tried to bring out the emotion that there is in Holmes. On the surface he seems a cold, sometimes dark, rather off-putting figure. But deeper down, I think, he is a man of feeling.

'He is complex. He loves music – he plays the violin very well – he enjoys a joke, he is vain, maybe a little conceited. He likes to be praised. He can be bitchy when he assesses other great detectives.

'He can be a bit of a drama queen; he shows off sometimes, he's something of an exhibitionist, especially when he has pulled off a coup.

'On a difficult case he may build up considerable tension within himself, which explodes in a genial bit of theatricality when the problem is solved.

'I've tried to get some of that into my Holmes.

'That's why of all the stories I've done for Granada my favourite is *The Naval Treaty*: it was the first in which I felt I could be a bit of me as well as Holmes. I wore a beige suite and a straw hat. I was allowed to laugh, and at the end, when Holmes knew he'd cracked the problem, I made him do a little skip and dance. Some viewers may not have approved, but for me it was a breakthrough.

'The programme I'm most proud of? That's a different matter. Again, personal: *The Sign of Four*.

'It was very demanding because it's a full length film with a great number of varied scenes – tremendous action. I wasn't in normal health at the time, and in particular, I had to do a lot of walking about on roofs, and I've no head for heights. I was pleased with myself when I got through that film in one piece.

'Playing Holmes for five years is hard going, but it's done me sterling service. I'm very grateful. When I do my shopping, people stop and talk to me. You have the feeling that the hard work you've done has not gone unappreciated. A good feeling.

'It's good to feel that the work done by your colleagues has been appreciated. When Mike Cox dreamed up this series there was no great enthusiasm about it. Nobody spoke of it as a guaranteed success. Many different people had to put their best into it for a long time before it was clear that it was a hit.

'I could give you a long list of the people who slogged to get the series off the ground; Mike Grimes who planned and built the sets; June Wyndham Davies, the producer, who polishes each film till it's like a diamond; Gordon Pleasant and Claire McCourt, the stage managers, and my dresser, Don Sayer.

'And that's naming just a few.

'But the people who work on the set are every bit as important. Above all, the electricians. There's no sun in this country. Practically everything you shoot has to be lit. And lighting in this country demands immense skill, patience and real dedication to the job.

'My ambition for the future is to tour the world, to save enough pennies to buy my own theatre in London, and put on a variety of productions, some, I hope, which I'll have sorted out in various countries on the world tour.

'I'm going to try to give something back to the profession which has been so good to me, provide work for some of the young who are unemployed. Not forgetting the electricians.'

'I am lost without my Boswell'

* * *

'Watson has some remarkable characteristics of his own, to which in his modesty he has given small attention amid his exaggerated estimates of my own performance'

* * *

DAVID BURKE *as Watson*

The two Watsons seen on Granada Television have differed greatly from those seen anywhere else before. They have been more convincing. Why? The first of them, David Burke, explains it this way: 'Because Watson is the narrator of the stories, he has little to say, and very little to do....the easiest way for Watson to get into the show is to be slightly funny. For this reason, I believe, many actors in the past fell into the trap of going overboard on the comedy'. How right he is: Watson is *not* a comic character. Tall, good-looking, vital, David Burke played Watson as Conan Doyle's text portrays him, a man who amply justifies Holmes's frequent tributes to him, such as, 'Watson has some remarkable characteristics of his own to which in his modesty he has given small attention amid his exaggerated estimates of my own performance'. Good for you, Holmes, and good for David Burke, who, drawing on wide experience ranging from Shakespeare to contemporary West End Theatre, pioneered the *proper* Watson.

'I know, my dear Watson, that you share my love of all that is bizarre and outside the conventions and humdrum routine of everyday life'

THE TWO WATSONS

EDWARD HARDWICKE *as Watson*

Edward Hardwicke modestly says that when he was offered the chance of succeeding David Burke as Watson his reaction was: 'Oh, God, have I got to follow that. You see, David had been absolutely marvellous'. But he took up the challenge – he and Burke were good friends – and made such a contribution of his own, for instance by portaying Watson as an older man, that he can be said to have completed the role's rehabilitation. He had striking qualifications. Nigel Bruce, one of the most famous Watsons ever, was a great friend of Sir Cedric Hardwicke, Edward's father, who played Sherlock Holmes in a famous radio series. Edward's experience has been remarkably varied. Beginning in Malvern at the age of seven, a year later in Hollywood he played opposite Spencer Tracy in *A Guy named Joe*. In the RAF he did a two-man comedy act with Ronnie Corbett. There followed three years at the Bristol Old Vic; seven with the National Theatre; and many appearances in ITV. His success in interpreting Watson, like David Burke's, comes from his insight into that unique personality whom Holmes described as 'the one fixed point in a changing age'.

* * *

'I never get your limits, Watson...there are unexplored possibilities about you'

* * *

'Oh, a trusty comrade is always of use. And a chronicler still more so'

'...the lowest and vilest alleys...' –

THE LONDON OF HOLMES

'Look out of this window, Watson... the thief or the murderer could roam London on such a day as the tiger does the jungle, unseen until he pounces, and then evident only to his victim'

LOCATING 221B Baker Street remains a problem. Most of the experts agree about one thing: Holmes did not live where 221B would be today, at the north end of the street, opposite the west entrance to the Baker Street Underground station.

The most important clue to the site of 221B is in *The Empty House*, the story in which we discover that Holmes did not after all fall to his death in the Reichenbach Falls but is back in business in London.

The clue is Watson's detailed description of the streets and mews in the detour which, in order not to be spotted by Moriarty's men, he and Holmes made by night and by stealth to get from Cavendish Square to *The Empty House* in Baker Street, immediately opposite 221B.

In the front room of the empty house, in the dark, crouched the ferocious Colonel Moran, dedicated to avenging Dr Moriarty, who *did* fall to his death in the Reichenbach Falls. The Colonel, a disgrace to the British army, intended to put a bullet through Holmes's skull as he sat – so Moran thought, but he was looking at a dummy, – in his first-floor sitting-room opposite. Identify *The Empty House* and we can locate 221B. Elementary, my dear Watson.

The majority of the experts favour two sites for 221B. The first is Number 109 or 111, next door to each other, on the west side of the northern part of Baker Street, a few yards south of the Marylebone Road. The second is Number 31, also on the west side of Baker Street, but much further south towards Oxford Street, now part of a modern office block.

There is also the view that 221B stood on the *east* side of Baker Street at its corner with George Street, while the researchers for the Granada television series, after painstaking study, came to the conclusion that 221B was indeed on the east side of Baker Street but much further north, roughly opposite 109.

'It is a hobby of mine to have an exact knowledge of London', says Holmes in *The Red-Headed League*, and he certainly seemed to enjoy showing his 'exact knowledge' off. In *The Sign of Four*, for example, he accompanies the lovely Miss Morstan and Watson on their journey in a four-wheeler from the Lyceum Theatre at the corner of Exeter Street and Wellington Street, off the Strand, WC2, across the river to somewhere in Stockwell, SW9. According to Watson, he reels off the names of all the streets on the way.

This performance can only be described as miraculous. The distance must have been close to three miles, and we have Watson's word for it that the night was so foggy that even in the well-lit Strand 'the lamps were but misty splotches of diffused light, which threw a feeble circular glimmer upon the slimy pavement'.

Holmes's eyesight must have been infra-red.

Even so, he was unable to name the street in which the house they sought was situated, the home of Mr Thaddeus Sholto, possibly No 3 Milkwood Road, SE24. Watson says it was 'a new terrace'.

Had Holmes's 'exact knowledge' failed him? And had the protective Watson tried to excuse him by claiming that this street was new?

Be that as it may, when later that night they drove on to Norwood, and Holmes might have treated us to another running commentary, we do not hear a word from him; it is Mr Thaddeus Sholto who eventually announces 'Pondicherry Lodge'.

This, the residence of Thaddeus's twin brother, Bartholomew, murdered just before they arrived – Holmes did not always arrive in the nick of time – was a house very similar to The Rookery, Streatham Common.

THE STRAND

This long drive through the night and the fog took Holmes and Watson very far from their stamping ground in the centre of the metropolis.

Mentions of Oxford Street are numerous since Holmes and Watson lived only a short walk away and shopped there. (Conan Doyle once practised in Devonshire Place, very near Harley Street, also within easy walking distance.)

Three hundred yards off Oxford Circus is the site of the former Langham Hotel, once the most exclusive and fashionable hotel in London. It figures in several stories. In *A Scandal in Bohemia*, the King of that country was in residence there. Later, it was taken over for offices by the BBC, whose headquarters are across the street in Portland Place.

Regent Street, leading off Oxford Street to the South, is frequently cited, as is Piccadilly Circus at the southern end of it. It was here, at the bar of the Criterion in the early 1880s, that Watson bumped into his old friend, Stamford, who was at lunch at the Holborn Restaurant, which once stood at the west corner of Kingsway and High Holborn, and told him about a Mr Sherlock Holmes, who was looking for somebody who would share digs with him. That afternoon Watson was introduced to Holmes at St Bartholomew's Hospital, 'Bart's', where Holmes was doing some research.

The Strand is particularly evocative in Holmesian lore. First, many of the Holmes stories appeared in the *Strand Magazine*, published from Southampton Street, just off the Strand.

Secondly, the Strand is mentioned many times in the stories.

In *The Hound of the Baskervilles*, Sir Henry of that ilk buys a pair of boots which plays an important part in the mystery. He probably purchased them at the shop of G.H.Harris in the Strand.

Holmes and Watson dined frequently at Simpson's, famous for its roast beef.

In *The Final Problem* Watson hurried to the Strand in a hansom – the one-horse cab driven from behind the roof which Disraeli called 'the gondola of London' – to be picked up by a mysterious brougham

VICTORIA STATION

and driven (by Holmes's brother Mycroft in disguise) to meet Holmes at Victoria Station en route for the drama at the Reichenbach Falls.

Watson knew the Strand well. Having been invalided home from India, 'struck on the shoulder by a Jezail bullet' – in some stories it seems to have worked its way down to his leg – he lived there for a time in a private hotel.

LONDON BRIDGE

The Trafalgar Square end of the Strand runs into Northumberland Avenue where once stood the Northumberland Hotel. This is where Sir Henry Baskerville's new boot was stolen. It is now 'The Sherlock Holmes' pub and restaurant where you can dine and look through a glass screen into a most entertaining reproduction of the sitting room in 221B.

In *The Illustrious Client* Holmes and Watson came to the Turkish Baths in Northumberland Avenue. According to Holmes's brother Mycroft in *The Greek Interpreter* there were many hotels in the Avenue which catered for 'wealthy Orientals'.

Mycroft should have known, since, apart from the fact that he knew everything, his lodgings, in Pall Mall, and his club, the Diogenes (probably the Athenaeum) were within a few minutes' walking distance.

Also off the Strand was Covent Garden where Holmes loved to relax enjoying both sung and instrumental music, 'sometimes', according to Watson, 'gently waving his long thin fingers in time to the music'. Watson seems to have had no objection to this behaviour, but the Garden would have been unbearable if every other music buff had done the same.

Nearby is Covent Garden market, which Holmes went to on a goose chase which turned out to be far from wild in *The Blue Carbuncle*.

Close by was Bow Street Police Station headed by Inspector Bradstreet of *The Man with the Twisted Lip*, one of Holmes's admirers.

The north end of the Strand runs into Fleet Street, then as now, though less so, the street of newspapers. It features in *The Redheaded League* and in *The Resident Patient*. In the former, 'Pope's Court' may have been Mitre Court between Fleet Street and the Temple.

THE TERRACE, HOUSE OF COMMONS

THE UNDERGROUND, BAKER STREET

South-east of the Strand and roughly parallel to it is the Thames Embankment where the body of John Openshaw was discovered in *The Five Orange Pips*.

Some of the stories deal very specifically with places. For instance, the centre of the action in *The Norwood Builder* is the home of the missing Jonas Oldacre, 'a big modern villa of staring brick', in Lower Norwood about ten miles south of Trafalgar Square.

The Norwood area of south London appears several times in the stories. Conan Doyle lived in 12, Tennison Road, South Norwood for a number of years.

Much of the action in *A Scandal in Bohemia* is in and around Irene Adler's residence, Briony Lodge, Serpentine Avenue, St John's Wood, 'a bijou villa, with a garden at the back...in a small street in a quiet neighbourhood' reports Holmes. This time *he* sounds like an estate agent.

Some of the centres of action, notably the house of Charles Augustus Milverton, 'the worst man in London...the king of all the blackmailers', are not so well pin-pointed.

'Appledore Towers' was in Hampstead, on or very near the Heath. It may have been the big house on the heath at the fork of Spaniards Road with North End Road, or 'the silent gloomy house' off the heath at the corner of East Heath Road and Well Road, later known as 'The Logs'.

COVENT GARDEN

The story of *The Six Napoleons* takes Holmes to several houses, including: Pitt Street, Kensington, 'a quiet little backwater just beside one of the briskest currents of London life', this particular current being Kensington High Street; Church Street, Stepney, in the East End of London, 'river-side city of a hundred thousand souls, where the tenement houses swelter and reek with the outcasts of Europe'; and Laburnham Vale, Chiswick, just off the river, not far from the south end of Hammersmith Bridge, 'a secluded road fringed with pleasant houses, each standing in its own ground'.

NORTHUMBERLAND AVENUE

OXFORD CIRCUS

According to Watson, the ghastly East End opium den he visited in *The Man with the Twisted Lip* was 'The Bar of Gold' in Upper Swandam Lane, 'a vile alley lurking behind the high wharves which line the north side of the river to the north side of London Bridge'.

There is no such lane; most of the experts think Watson had in mind Lower Thames Street, which runs along and close to the Thames from London Bridge nearly to the Tower.

LIMEHOUSE

Holmes told Watson that the 'Bar of Gold' was 'the vilest murder-trap in London', innumerable bodies having been taken out of it via 'a trapdoor....near the corner of Paul's Wharf'. There *is* a Paul's Wharf, and though it is not where Holmes says it was, it certainly looks as if it might have got rid of some bodies in its time.

Whether or not Holmes was boasting a bit when he claimed 'an exact knowledge of London' there is no doubt that he loved the city. 'The evening has brought a breeze with it,' he says to Watson at the beginning of *The Resident Patient*, adding 'What about a ramble through London?'

Watson records: 'For three hours we strolled about together, watching the ever-changing kaleidoscope of life as it ebbs and flows through Fleet Street and the Strand. It was ten o'clock before we reached Baker Street again'.

Do we deduce that Fleet Street and the Strand was Holmes's favourite part of London? Or did he leave it to Watson to choose where they would go?

FLEET STREET

Whichever, there is something engaging and endearing about the thought of these two old friends sauntering along through the heart of their beloved London, leisurely exchanging comments on the humanity around them, and, ready for bed, returning to Baker Street – only to find another exciting mystery awaiting them.

JOHN BEVAN
TORQUAY
CIVILITY
&
PROMPT
PAYMENT

'...the smiling and beautiful countryside'.

HOLMES OUT OF LONDON

SHERLOCK HOLMES has a curious idea of the geography of the country of his birth, or, at any rate, of where the 'north' of England was. In *The Priory School* he speaks of 'Mackleton, in the North of England,' when Matlock, on which Mackleton is based, is in the county of Derbyshire, in the Midlands.

In *The Gloria Scott* Holmes visits Donnithorpe, a hamlet (fictitious) in Norfolk. He says he 'set out for the north.' Norfolk is in East Anglia. In the opinion of a leading Holmes expert, the late Lord Gore-Booth, 'for Holmes the north began some 120 miles from London in a generally northerly direction. Alas, it begins there for many British citizens today.'

This reference to the 'north' comes from Holmes's own lips. Such a cavalier attitude to geography cannot be blamed on Watson.

Sherlock Holmes, as he told us in *A Study in Scarlet*, considered that a man's brain should not be lumbered with 'useless facts elbowing out the useful ones'. This may explain why his knowledge of the lower half of England is much more reliable than his knowledge of the upper half; most of his cases originated there.

Or Holmes may have learned from his mistakes. When in *The Dancing Men* he entrains for Ridling Thorpe Manor, not far from North Walsham, in Norfolk, he does not say he 'set out for the north.' Perhaps by now he had consulted a map, or had asked Watson where the north *was*.

The countryside which most dominates any of the Holmes stories is Dartmoor in the county of Devon, the eerie background to the action in *The Hound of the Baskervilles*.

This is the West Country. Dartmoor is about 180 miles as the crow flies west-south-west of London. Approaching it in the train, Watson beheld 'a grey melancholy hill, with a strange jagged summit', the hill probably being the famous Brent Tor. Watson, seeing the Tor for the first time, mistook for a 'jagged summit' the church of St Michael of the Rock which stands on the top. He should have checked.

Baskerville Hall may be Lew House (or Hall) at Lew Trenchard, near Lew Down, Devon. The nearby hamlet of Grimpen is probably Widecombe-in-the-Moor, once famous for Widecombe Fair and Tom Pearse's grey mare. Three miles distant lies 'Grimspound Bog', the 'Great Grimpen Mire' of the story.

Experts have asked why Conan Doyle called it a mire instead of a bog. One answer is that Conan Doyle, delicate to a fault, avoided the use of the word 'bog', a slang term among schoolboys for 'lavatory'.

Holmes made another visit to Devon in *Silver Blaze,* the mystery of the kidnapped racehorse trained at King's Pyland Stables, Dartmoor, two miles east of Tavistock, probably near Princetown, the site of the prison (real) mentioned in *The Hound of the Baskervilles.*

Silver Blaze contains the most famous of all Holmesian exchanges:

The Police Inspector to Holmes: 'Is there any other point to which you would wish to draw my attention?'

BRENT TOR

'To the curious incident of the dog in the night-time'.

'The dog did nothing in the night-time'.

'That was the curious incident,' remarked Sherlock Holmes.

Holmes went even further west, into Cornwall, to solve the problem of *The Devil's Foot*. The horrific episode had occurred in a house described as 'Tredannick Wartha' near a hamlet called 'Tredannick Wollas'. Conan Doyle may have had Predannack Wollas and Cwry in mind both near Poldhu Bay. The story? A real Cornish nasty.

Holmes went West again, though this time to a different part of it, to the neighbourhood of Ross, in Herefordshire – picturesque fishing country along the banks of the Wye. Here he swiftly cleared up *The Boscombe Valley Mystery*.

Many people point out that the Boscombe we know of is on the northern border of the western county of Somerset. You can't please everybody.

Notwithstanding these forays into the West Country, the highest incidence of Holmes's cases are to be found much nearer to Baker Street: in Sussex and Surrey.

To solve the mystery of *The Musgrave Ritual* Holmes went to the home of the Musgrave family, 'the manor house of Hurlstone...perhaps the oldest inhabited building in the county' of Sussex, in reality, perhaps, the manor house of West Hoathly.

Also in Sussex was Wisteria Lodge, situated between Esher and Oxshott, an unlikely venue for Voodooism. For *The Sussex Vampire* Holmes went to Cheeseman's, an 'isolated and ancient farmhouse'

MITRE HOTEL, OXFORD

near Lamberley, neither of which places exists, both, according to Watson, situated south of Horsham, which does.

Holmes solved several cases in Surrey. For *The Crooked Man* he went to Aldershot; for *The Solitary Cyclist* to Charlington, near Farnham, the mystery developing in the vicinity of 'Crooksbury Hill', most likely Monk's Hill, part of Crooksbury Common.

It was in Surrey, too, that the terrifying events of *The Speckled Band* took place *chez* Dr Grimesby Roylott, at Stoke Moran, three miles from Leatherhead, in beautiful country. Conan Doyle most probably had Stoke D'Abernon in mind. The Manor House, in which Dr Roylott dwelt, seems to have been situated between Slyfield House and Woodlands Park. Some implausibilities in this story, but there can be no doubt that Dr Roylott should have been struck off the medical register.

There is some argument about the location of 'Briarbrae', Woking, in *The Naval Treaty*, also in Surrey.

Described as 'a large detached house standing in extensive grounds, within a few minutes' walk of the station...' it could have been Woodham Hall, but more likely was Inchcape House, now destroyed.

CHRIST CHURCH

Judging by the photographs, this may have been no great loss.

Holmes made several visits to Kent, notably, in *The Golden Pince-Nez*, to Yoxley Old Place, 'down in Kent, seven miles from Chatham'. Nobody knows of that old pile, but there is a Yoxley Old Hall near Bury St Edmunds in Suffolk, which, like Norfolk, is in East Anglia. There is no evidence that Holmes got the two confused.

Bedford is a market town on the River Ouse situated in Bedfordshire. A few miles away, according to Watson, is Tuxbury Old Hall where they went in the case of *The Blanched Soldier*; 'a great wandering house...starting on a half-timbered

ROSS-ON-WYE

Elizabethan foundation and ending in a Victorian portico'. Awful house, good story.

For *The Problem of Thor Bridge*, Holmes had to go down to the country of Hampshire, not far from Winchester, where, in the middle of a well-wooded and extensive estate, stood Thor Place.

According to Watson this was as 'wide-spread, half-timbered house, half Tudor and half Georgian' reached by 'a walk of half a mile or so across a wind-swept heath, all gold and bronze with the fading ferns'. If Watson had failed as a biographer he could have become an estate agent.

To get to grips with *The Creeping Man* Holmes put up at one of our two ancient Universities in a

PRINCETOWN PRISON

famous hotel he called 'The Chequers'. Most experts favour Oxford and 'The Mitre'.

Holmesian scholars continue to debate whether Holmes was a student at Oxford or at Cambridge, or at neither or at both. The majority view is that he went to Christ Church, Oxford.

At least one case took Holmes to Cambridge, *The Missing Three Quarter*. In search of the absconded Rugger Blue he scoured the lovely villages of Cambridgeshire, his quest culminating in Trumpington.

There came a day when as he says in *The Lion's Mane* Sherlock Holmes retired; to 'my little Sussex home...my villa is situated on the southern slope of the Downs, commanding a great view of the Channel'. He seems to have lived on the edge of the cliff above the beach.

However, in the final case, *His Last Bow*, Watson says to Holmes: 'We heard of you as living the life of a hermit among your bees and your books in a small farm upon the South Downs'. Holmes responds: 'Exactly, Watson'.

Is it possible to live 'on the southern slope of the Downs' and '*upon* the South Downs' at the same time? Or had Holmes moved house, bees and all, from one place to another? Or was this the final case of his careless attitude to geography?

In what mood did Holmes retire to the countryside?

'It is my belief, Watson, founded upon my experience, that the lowest and vilest alleys in London do not present a more dreadful record of sin than does the smiling and beautiful countryside'

In *Black Peter*, which took Holmes down to Woodman's Lee, possibly Coleman's Hatch, near Forest Row in Sussex, he says: 'Let us walk in these beautiful woods, Watson, and give a few hours to the birds and the flowers'. (The bees, presumably, were still to come).

But in *The Copper Beeches*, that story of the sinister house lying five miles 'on the far side of Winchester' in Hampshire, Holmes says: 'It is my belief, Watson, founded upon my experience, that the lowest and vilest alleys in London do not present a more dreadful record of sin than does the smiling and beautiful countryside'.

Could it be that having cleaned up London Holmes got bored, and moved out of town to find a new challenge in the countryside?

Irene Adler – '*the* woman', Holmes always called her – who could have caused *A Scandal in Bohemia*: played by Gayle Hunnicut.

Mrs Hudson, of No. 221b Baker Street, Sherlock Holmes's loyal and devoted – but often exasperated – landlady: played by Rosalie Williams.

The LADIES

WE HAVE it in *The Second Stain*, straight from Sherlock Holmes's own mouth: 'Now, Watson, the fair sex is your department.' And all the ladies in the Holmes stories, even the unpleasant ones, get a brief but specific description from the Doctor, and for many of the attractive ones, it is clear, John Watson's heart beats a little faster.

On the other hand, Watson has made out that Sherlock Holmes was incapable of love for woman. In *A Scandal in Bohemia* Watson says: 'All emotions, and that one particularly, were abhorrent to his cold, precise, but admirably balanced mind...He never spoke of the softer passions, save with a gibe and a sneer.'

Lady Hilda Trelawney Hope,
beautiful, blackmailed, distraught:
she begged Holmes for help in
The Second Stain:
played by Patricia Hodge.

Miss Violet Hunter,
who became governess 'on curious
conditions', and saw strange
things at *The Copper Beeches*:
played by Natasha Richardson.

Lady Brackenstall,
'so womanly a presence'; her brutal husband
was murdered in *The Abbey Grange*:
played by Anne Louise Lambert.

Miss Helen Stoner,
terrified by her sister's mysterious death,
fears her own in *The Speckled Band*:
played by Rosalyn Landor.

Jeremy Kemp as *Dr Grimesby Roylott*

Patrick Newell as *Blessington*

Jeremy Brett as *Holmes* with Eric Porter as *Professor Moriarty*

VILLAINS

'You can tell an old master by the sweep of his brush. I can tell a Moriarty when I see one'

CONAN DOYLE was not only a splendid teller of tales, he was a prolific creator of characters. The men and women in his historical novels, a varied throng, of high and low rank and of miscellaneous professions, are all flesh and blood, something not easy to achieve in writing about the distant past.

The Sherlock Holmes stories, long and short, also abound in vivid convincing characters. Apart from the ever present central figure, and his faithful biographer, and a few others, who recur from time to time, like Mrs Hudson and Inspector Lestrade, all the men and women who come and go in these immortal pages are as different as they are real. Whether they are cab drivers, clerks, governesses, shopkeepers, musicians, city men, country squires or international statesmen they are all authentic.

None of Conan Doyle's writings provide a more mixed and colourful collection than the Sherlock Holmes villains. Here are eleven of them.

Jeremy Brett as Holmes with Eric Porter as Professor Moriarty. 'He is the Napoleon of Crime, Watson...the organizer of half that is evil and of nearly all that is undetected in this great city.' So said Holmes in *The Final Problem*, ten days or so before the most villainous villain of them all makes

Joss Ackland as *Jephro Rucastle*

Nicholas Gecks and Alan Howard as *James Wilder* and the *Duke of Holdernesse*

Ken Campbell as *James Ryder*

Rosalie Crutchley as *Mrs Lexington*

Yves Beneyton as *Eduardo Lucas*

the mistake of wrestling with Holmes on the edge of a precipice and plunges hundreds of feet to his death at the bottom of the Reichenbach Falls.

Jeremy Kemp as Dr Grimesby Roylott, of Stoke Moran, in *The Speckled Band*. If anybody looked a villain he certainly did. A horrible man, and it's no surprise when as a result of his mysterious machinations, this cold-blooded murderer dies as he intended his step-daughter to die, a case of the biter bit.

Joss Ackland as Jephro Rucastle, in *The Copper Beeches*. This inhuman schemer seemed 'a round jovial man...a very kind, goodnatured man' until he realised his wicked plot might be twigged, whereupon, 'in an instant the smile hardened into a grin of rage' and he threatened to throw his child's governess to his monstrous mastiff.

Patrick Newell as Blessington in *The Resident Patient*, on whom his double-crossed partners in crime avenged themselves by hanging him from a hook in the ceiling. A treacherous fellow. 'He was trying to hide his own identity from everybody as long as he could. His secret was a shameful one...' Holmes unmasked him and revealed all.

Nicholas Gecks and Alan Howard as James Wilder and the Duke of Holdernesse in *The Priory School*. Wilder, his secretary, snatches the Duke's infant son and heir from his dormitory and becomes an accessory to murder. Not a *deep-dyed* villain: so when he 'made a complete confession, so filled was he with horror and remorse', Holmes turned a blind eye and allowed him to emigrate to Australia.

Ken Campbell as James Ryder in *The Blue Carbuncle*. Ryder, seen here with the geese which figured so prominently in his plot, also was a light-weight villain compared to the others, and was certainly the luckiest, for Holmes having proved his guilt let him get away scott free. 'This fellow will not go wrong again; he is too terribly frightened', he said to Watson. Besides, it was Christmas.

George Costigan, as Wilson Kemp in *The Greek Interpreter*. This villain was a particularly nasty customer. 'A man of the foulest of antecedents... he spoke in a jerky, nervous fashion, and with some giggling laughs in between...The terror of his face lay in his eyes, however, steel grey, and glistening coldly, with a malevolent, inexorable cruelty in their depths.' Another kidnapper, but this one came to a sticky end.

Rosalie Crutchley as Mrs Lexington, the housekeeper in *The Norwood Builder*. She was 'a little, dark, silent person, with suspicious and sidelong eyes...as close as wax'. She abetted her awful employer in very nearly bringing an innocent man to the gallows. Holmes got on to the case only just in time.

James Hazeldine as Brunton, the butler in *The Musgrave Ritual*, who, 'a bit of a Don Juan', broke several ladies' hearts, was disgraced and dismissed, then disappeared until Holmes, by one of his most dramatic and complex feats of deduction, saw what the butler saw, and revealed 'his dreadful end'.

Yves Beneyton as Eduardo Lucas, the blackmailer in *The Second Stain*. One of the most charming men, and one of the best amateur tenors in the country, this smiling villain got his hands on a letter, publication of which would have involved Britain 'in a great war' and the Foreign Secretary in utter ruin. Holmes retrieved it in the nick of time. Lucas too died a violent death.

Patrick Allen as Colonel Sebastian Moran who in *The Empty House* killed the Hon Robert Adair with an air gun, not an ordinary one but a specially constructed air rifle firing expanding bullets, and then tried to kill Holmes in the same way. After Moriarty, whose lieutenant he was, 'the second most dangerous man in London', according to Holmes. Career: Eton, Oxford, and Indian Army. Starting 'with great capacities for good or for evil', Moran had gone to the bad. Now, bumping into Holmes, he goes to the gallows.

George Costigan as *Wilson Kemp*

James Hazeldine as *Brunton*

Patrick Allen as *Colonel Sebastian Moran*

A Dual Centenary?

Jack the Ripper & Sherlock Holmes

THE appearance of Sherlock Holmes, in *A Study in Scarlet*, coincided with the most famous series of murders in British history, those committed by the mysterious 'Jack the Ripper'.

Some experts claim that five murders only, committed in 1888, were the work of 'The Ripper'. Others maintain that his ghastly work began earlier.

What Sherlock Holmes is in fictional crime, Jack the Ripper is in real crime – legendary, and in a class by himself.

The Ripper may well have helped pave the way for Sherlock Holmes's fame. His murders headlined unsolved crime as never before. People longed for some brilliant sleuth to emerge and catch this elusive terror.

People in pubs and in their homes speculated, often in hushed voices, about who the Ripper might be. Thousands tried to detect, reason and deduce as Sherlock Holmes did. There was no cinema, radio or TV in 1888; people talked about crime instead of watching it on horror films and thrillers.

Many aspects of the Ripper crimes caught the public imagination: the skill and nerve of the killer; the violence of the assault; the frightful things done to some of the victims; the belief that the murderer had a knowledge of anatomy, and was an educated man; the apparent absence of motive.

But what above all most fascinated and frightened the public was that nobody was brought to trial. To this day nobody can say for sure who the murderer was.

He may have committed other murders, but five murders only are accepted beyond question as the work of the Ripper. They were carried out between 31 August and 9 November 1888, within easy walking distance of each other in the Whitechapel area in the East End of London.

The victims were prostitutes. Four were middle-aged, drunken, and by no means attractive. The fifth was twenty-five, attractive but also drunken, and, like the others, 'on the road to ruin'.

All five had had their throats cut. Four had been mutilated. In the case of the second woman some of the entrails had been removed and were left beside the body, which like the other three, was found in the street.

The fifth woman, the only one killed indoors, had been terribly mutilated, and then carved up into portions as though by a butcher. The kidneys, heart and other organs were laid out on a table beside the victim's bed, as though on a stall.

The murders caused a public outcry unusual at a time when violent crime in the East End was a byword. There were editorials in *The Times* and questions in Parliament. The police came in for unprecedented criticism.

After the fifth murder, there were no more killings that looked like the Ripper's handiwork. No more characteristic 'Ripper' letters arrived at Scotland Yard.

A few weeks later, 31 December, the body of a man was retrieved from the Thames. The police said they were sure that this was the corpse of Jack the Ripper and that he had committed suicide soon after the last murder. The hunt for the murderer was consequently called off.

The body was that of Montague John Druitt, aged thirty-one. His appearance answered closely to that of a description given by a person who saw one of the murdered women talking to a man who may have been the Ripper just before her death.

Druitt was not a doctor, but he was grandson, son, nephew and cousin of doctors, and had access to surgical instruments.

Motive? A note found with the body said his mother was insane, and he feared he was becoming insane himself. The theory was that in his near madness he blamed her for his condition, and sought revenge by slaughtering women who symbolised her, disembowelling them as a ghastly protest against the vital process which had given him birth.

Proof? In so far as there is any, Druitt's own brother believed he had committed the murders, and so did the police.

But in his suicide note, if it was he who wrote it, Druitt did not confess to being the Ripper.

The theory that Druitt was the Ripper is fascinatingly outlined by Mr Daniel Farson in his book *Jack the Ripper* published in 1972.

Other theories point to other suspects. They include: a midwife; an eminent surgeon; another eminent surgeon; a mentally unbalanced Jewish ritual slaughterer; a Russian secret agent sent to London to commit murders to make the British police look foolish; the son of a Bloomsbury intellectual; a crazed Russian anarchist; a Polish immigrant; a religious maniac.

The most dramatic hypothesis, appearing in 1970, was put forward by a distinguished and octagenarian surgeon, and ventilated on television and radio.

According to this theory, the Ripper was Queen Victoria's grandson, Albert, the Duke of Clarence. Had he not died – in the 'flu' epidemic of 1892 – Albert, not George, would have presumably succeeded his father, Edward VII as king.

According to this theory, the youthful Duke had contracted syphilis during his years in the Navy, and, suffering the consequent mental derangement,

several times visited the East End to revenge himself on representatives of the sex which he might have supposed had transmitted the disease.

His knowledge of anatomy, the theory goes, could have been acquired by seeing deer being disembowelled and their carcasses dressed – maybe learning to do it himself – after stalking them in Scotland.

There is another theory involving the Duke of Clarence, but not as the Ripper. This was advanced by Mr Stephen Knight in his book *Jack the Ripper – The Final Solution*, published in 1976.

Mr Knight's theory, also discussed on radio and television, was based on extensive conversations with Joseph Sickert, son of the famous painter, Walter Sickert, who was a friend of the Duke of Clarence. Mr Knight claims that the information he

was given originated in what Joseph Sickert had been told many years previously by his father.

According to this account, the Duke of Clarence, a close friend of Walter Sickert, was a frequent visitor to his studio in Cleveland Street, which runs parallel to, and a couple of hundred yards west of, Tottenham Court Road.

Sickert's studio was at the centre of a bohemian, loose-living area, known for heterosexual and homosexual promiscuity, frequented by many well known public figures. Here the Duke of Clarence met a shop-girl whom the painter employed as a model, Annie Crook. He fell in love with her, married her, and had a daughter by her.

Queen Victoria and the prime minister, Lord Salisbury, learned of this. At this time, Republican feeling was growing, the Queen was unpopular, and there was public indignation about the sexual immorality of the Prince of Wales. The monarchy and the Conservative government felt insecure. Queen Victoria and her prime minister, Lord Salisbury, consequently were horrified to learn of the young Duke's indiscretion, the more so since the girl was a Catholic, this being a time of great anti-Catholic feeling.

Mr Knight's theory postulates that Salisbury ordered a raid on Cleveland Street, as a result of which the Duke was hauled off and kept under

'Is that "The Ripper", Watson?' – A contemporary artist seems to have used Holmes and Watson as his models.

The Duke of Clarence – His private life may have brought about the dreadful crimes.

Sir William Gull – Was he Jack the Ripper?

Montague Druitt – The police said he was 'The Ripper'.

supervision for the rest of his life, Annie being confined in a succession of workhouses and hospitals, dying in one thirty-two years later.

Mary Kelly, a friend of Annie Crook, and onetime nannie to the child, confided information of these events to at least three friends of hers, who were prostitutes, the coterie planning to use their knowledge for blackmail.

Salisbury now feared that there would be a disclosure which would burst like a bombshell on the political scene and perhaps bring down the government, if not the monarchy. The four prostitutes in the know – the fifth was destroyed in error – must be silenced.

Mr Knight's theory does not imply that Salisbury was to blame for the murders; all he wanted was silence. Mr Knight believes that the murders were carried out by men who knew what Salisbury wanted, thought murder the only way to achieve it, and acted on their own initiative.

These men were Sir William Gull, Physician in Ordinary to Queen Victoria; Sir Robert Anderson, an Assistant Commissioner of the Metropolitan Police; John Netley, a coachman who owned his own vehicle, in which he had frequently driven the Duke of Clarence on his secret visits to Cleveland Street.

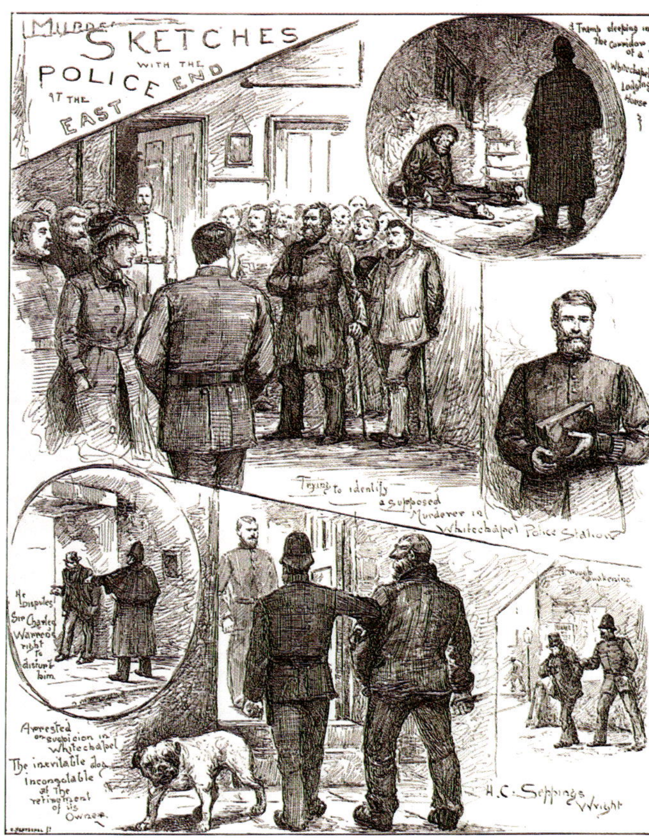

The Illustrated London News, 22 September, 1888.

Gull and Anderson, says Mr Knight, were dedicated Freemasons, bound to one another by oaths of loyalty and secrecy. They were members of the same lodge as Lord Salisbury. The women were murdered according to the Masonic ritual.

Four of them were killed in the coach. (That there was so little blood on the pavements on which the first four bodies were discoverd was much commented upon.)

According to Mr Knight, Walter Sickert knew all about the murders, was an accessory, and may have participated himself – he possessed a case of surgical knives.

There is no end it seems to theorising about the identity of Jack the Ripper. In 1987 two new books appeared: "The Bloody Truth" by Melvin Harris and "The Ripper Legacy" by Martin Howells and Keith Skinner.

The *proven* identity of the Ripper remains a mystery.

Sherlock Holmes did in fact 'meet' The Ripper in the film *Murder by Decree*, 1978

The Art of Detection

'Crime is common. Logic is rare. Therefore it is upon the logic rather than the crime that you should dwell'

'Is there any other point which I can make clear?'

SHERLOCK HOLMES was more often than not extremely critical of the methods and intelligence of the police, but, bearing in mind his vanity, and the fact that Scotland Yard inspectors were so often critical of *him*, we should not conclude that the Metropolitan Police of 1890 were a bunch of morons.

Having said that, and without going on to idolise Sherlock Holmes, it has to be said that he brought into the world of detection techniques and ideas which were peculiarly his own, and which he was, with all the generosity of a great creative genius, only too happy to share with all others in the trade.

Holmes was very scientific. The use of the magnifying glass, the litmus paper, the microscope, the retort boiling above the bunsen burner, were part of his repertoire. He could read foot-prints like a book, and tell whether a man was walking or running, limping, staggering, or carrying a heavy weight. He was familiar with the treads of different bicycle tyres.

Not only could he do these things but he could, and does, tell the reader how to do them too.

Unlike the Scotland Yard detectives of his period he had the time to build up and record a considerable body of scientific expertise, much of which he published in what he called his 'Monographs'. Though these were intensively researched treatises, his references to them were modest: for example, he describes 'The Typewriter and its Relation to Crime' as 'another little monograph'.

All kinds of type were grist to Holmes's mill, as is clear from what he says about newspaper type faces in *The Hound of the Baskervilles*.

Holmes also wrote two monographs on 'The Human Ear', which, he claims, were published in *The Anthropological Journal* in 1898. Others were: 'Upon the Distinction Between the Ashes of the Various Tobaccos'; 'Upon the Tracing of Footsteps'; 'Upon the Influences of a Trade Upon the Form of the Hand'.

'There is no one who knows the higher criminal world of London so well as I do'

There was another monograph which Holmes mentioned in *The Dancing Men*, entitled 'Upon Secret Writings'.

According to the experts, Holmes may have written other monographs, on, for example, tattooing. But enough of all that for now; clearly

'The pipe was still between his lips'

'Detection is, or ought to be, an exact science'

'"My collection of M's is a fine one," said he'

'You know my method. It is founded upon the observance of trifles'

'You know, Watson, I don't mind confessing to you that I have always had an idea that I would have made a highly efficient criminal'

*

'It is a capital mistake to theorize before you have all the evidence'

'Holmes held up the paper'

he thought it important to collate information which he thought might help to fight crime.

The foregoing does not mean that Holmes was out of touch with the day to day realities of the detective's life. We know that at least once he carried a dark lantern and a set of burglar's tools. Watson was asked from time to time to take his revolver with him. Scotland Yard inspectors were on more than one occasion advised to have their handcuffs ready.

Two of several methods separated Holmes from the detectives of Scotland Yard.

First: when he was presented with a mystery, instead of proceeding with a painstaking routine inquiry, interviewing all witnesses, all possible suspects, writing everything down in his notebook, he would extend his antennae, hoping to pick up one or more salient facts which would put him on the scent. Consequently, he often noted something which nobody else had seen. An outstanding example of this occurs in *Silver Blaze*. The inspector says 'The dog did nothing in the night-time'. Sherlock Holmes replies: 'That was the curious incident'.

'There's the scarlet thread of murder running through the colourless skein of life, and our duty is to unravel it, and isolate it, and expose every inch of it'

'I propose to devote my declining years to the composition of a textbook which shall focus the whole art of detection into one volume'

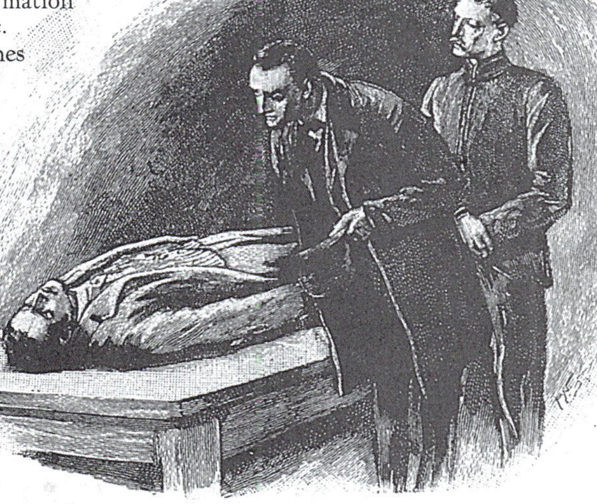

'There was no powder-blackening on the clothes'

'His eyes bent upon the glow of the fire'

Thus one of his main attractions for us: he continually informs us that if we *observe* as closely as he does what is right under our noses, we too can 'make important deductions'.

The other method which made Holmes different from the Scotland Yard detectives: he believed that by powerful deductive logic concentrated on reliable facts, it was possible if not to solve the problem at least to advance a long way along the road to doing so without even visiting the scene of the crime. Holmes exemplified this in *A Case of Identity*, *The Red-Headed League* and *The Noble Bachelor*, amongst others.

Many was the time when, everybody being baffled, Holmes would sit through the night smoking – 'this is a three pipe problem' – pondering deeply with all the force of his mighty mind, and come up with the solution, and his immortal comment: 'elementary'.

This, above all, is what gives him his unique place in our imagination. He is what we all like to be: The Armchair Detective.

'I am the last and highest court of appeal in detection'

HOLMES IN DISGUISES

AND SOME GROTESQUES

'My eyes have been trained to examine faces and not their trimmings. It is the first quality of a criminal investigator that he should see through a disguise'

IN *A Scandal in Bohemia,* Watson tells us, 'the door opened, and a drunken-looking groom, ill-kempt and side-whiskered with an inflamed face and disreputable clothes, walked into the room'.

The apparition must have looked much as Jeremy Brett does here. 'Accustomed as I was to my friend's amazing powers in the use of disguise', says Watson, 'I had to look three times before I was certain that it was indeed he'.

A Scandal in Bohemia Jeremy Brett

Holmes knew that to be successfully disguised one must be able to live as well as look the part. 'I lent the ostlers a hand in rubbing down their horses', he told the admiring Watson airily, 'and received as much information as I could desire...' about Irene Adler.

A quick-change artist as well as a master of disguise, Holmes 'then partook of some cold beef and a glass of beer', and changed into the 'amiable and simple-minded Nonconformist clergyman' whom Mr Brett also models on this page. Watson hastens to assure us: 'It was not merely that Holmes changed his costume. His expression, his manner, his very soul seemed to vary with every part that he assumed'.

Watson records other people's disguises also, notably the one with which the wealthy city man, Neville St Clair, passed himself off as the hideous beggar, Hugh Boone, seen here as played by Clive Francis in *The Man with the Twisted Lip.*

Watson had never seen such an ugly mug. 'A broad weal from an old scar ran across it from eye to chin, and by its contraction had turned up one side of the upper lip so that three teeth were exposed in a perpetual snarl'. Holmes deduced the real identity of the beggar Boone, and proved it by rubbing his face vigorously with a wet sponge. 'The man's face peeled off under the sponge like the bark from a tree'.

Watson did not admire everybody's attempts to disguise themselves. Indeed he seems positively critical of that of Carruthers in *The Solitary Cyclist,* seen here played by John Castle. 'That coal-black beard was in singular contrast to the pallor of his face', he observes, as though Carruthers was asking to be recognised, which indeed he was, the villainous Woodley 'with brutal and exultant laughter', shouting 'You can take your beard off, Bob. I know you well enough'. Poor show, Carruthers, Watson must have thought.

As well as disguised persons looking weird in the Holmes stories there are some undisguised persons looking pretty strange too: the grotesques. There are plenty in *The Sign of Four.* Thaddeus Sholto is one: 'a small man with a very high head, a bristle of red hair all round the fringe of it, and a bald, shining scalp which shot out from among it like a mountain peak from fir-trees. He writhed his hands together as he stood, and his features were in a perpetual jerk – now smiling, now scowling, but never for an instant in repose. Nature had given him a pendulous lip, and a too visible line of yellow and irregular teeth, which he strove feebly to conceal by constantly passing his hand over the lower part of his face'. Well, he did try.

Another collector's item in *The Sign of Four* was Jonathan Small, seen here as played by John Thaw, though his wooden leg doesn't show, accompanied by Tonga, the diminutive and imperfectly formed little beast from the Andaman Islands.

The Solitary Cyclist John Castle as CARRUTHERS

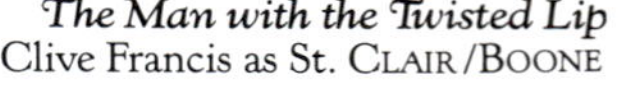

The Man with the Twisted Lip
Clive Francis as ST. CLAIR/BOONE

The Sign of Four
JONATHAN SMALL played by John Thaw and TONGA played by Kiran Shah

'form had filled out, his wrinkles were gone, the dull eyes had regained their fire', and there was Holmes. (Jeremy Brett again). 'It took me all my self-control to prevent me from breaking out into a cry of astonishment'.

Watson's self-control was exposed to an even stiffer test in *The Final Problem.* Boarding the boat train at Victoria he found in the reserved compartment not Holmes but 'a venerable Italian priest'. As the train moved off he heard the voice of Holmes. This time his self-control was not up to it. 'I turned in uncontrollable astonishment. The aged ecclesiastic had turned his face towards me. For an instant the wrinkles were smoothed away, the nose drew away from the chin, the lower lip ceased to protrude and the mouth to mumble, the dull eyes regained their fire, the drooping figure expanded. The next the whole frame had collapsed, and Holmes had gone as quickly as he had come. "Good heavens!" I cried. "How you startled me!"'

Watson wasn't kidding. These sudden appearances and disappearances of ostlers,

'Ah, you rogue!' cried Jones, highly delighted. 'You would have made an actor, and a rare one. You had the proper workhouse cough, and those weak legs of yours are worth ten pounds a week'

The Empty House
Jeremy Brett as the BOOKSELLER

The Man with the Twisted Lip
Jeremy Brett in the Opium Den

The Final Problem Jeremy Brett in disguise with David Burke as DR. WATSON

Small, says Watson, had 'a network of lines and wrinkles over his mahogany features...his heavy features and aggressive chin gave him a terrible expression when moved to anger'. As well as wearing a terrible expression when moved to anger, Mr Small hurled imprecations in 'a high, cracked voice'.

For Watson, the pygmy Tonga was the grotesque to end all grotesques, 'with a great misshapen head and a shock of tangled dishevelled hair. Never have I seen features so marked with all bestiality and cruelty...His small eyes glowed and burned with a sombre light, and his thick lips were writhed back from his teeth, which grinned and chattered at us with half-animal fury'. As well as looking like that, this pernicious pygmy sometimes killed people with poison darts puffed from a blow-pipe.

It is clear that such ghastly sights put quite a strain on Watson, but his nerves were also stretched by the rapidity with which Holmes donned and doffed his disguises. Threading his way through the bunks of a Limehouse opium den in *The Man with the Twisted Lip* Watson comes across an old man, 'very thin, very wrinkled, bent with age'. Suddenly he hears a familiar voice; momentarily the old man's nonconformist clergymen, elderly drug addicts and Italian priests, not to mention all the grotesques he was confronted with, were getting too much for him.

Things came to a head in *The Empty House.* Holmes had been posted missing presumed dead for years, almost certainly decomposing at the bottom of the Reichenbach Falls. Then an aged bookseller calls on Watson in Baker Street. One moment Watson is listening to this 'elderly deformed man...his sharp, wizened face peering out from a frame of white hair', rabbiting away 'in a strange croaking voice' about some tome on British Birds:

'A flush of colour sprang to Holmes's pale cheeks and he bowed to us like the master dramatist who receives the homage of his audience'

the next moment there is Holmes. No wonder poor Watson 'fainted for the first and last time in my life'.

Holmes had to bring him round with brandy. Note that as well as the first this was the *last* occasion on which Watson fainted. Either his nerves became conditioned to Holmes's quick-change acts or Holmes decided to give him more advance warning of them.

Or Watson may have decided to carry a hip-flask.

'After all, Watson, I am not retained by the police to supply their deficiencies'

'OLD BILL'

SHERLOCK HOLMES had a poor opinion of detectives as a class. He told Watson that Poe's famous sleuth, Dupin, was 'a very inferior fellow', and that Gaboriau's Lecoq was 'a miserable bungler'.

Watson felt 'rather indignant at having two characters whom I had admired treated in this cavalier style', and stalked over to the window and sulked. 'This fellow may be very clever', he said to himself, 'but he is certainly very conceited'.

It is only fair to say that at this time Watson had known Holmes only for a week, and did not yet know that his flat-mate was a detective, let alone the greatest ever.

Not surprisingly, Sherlock Holmes didn't think much of Lestrade, seen played by Colin Jeavons in *The Norwood Builder*, accompanied by a constable and about to make a typically fatuous arrest. The best Holmes could say of him was that with his sidekick Gregson he was 'the smartest of the Scotland Yarders...the pick of a bad lot'. They must have been a very bad lot indeed, since in *The Boscombe Valley Mystery* Lestrade is referred to as 'that imbecile'.

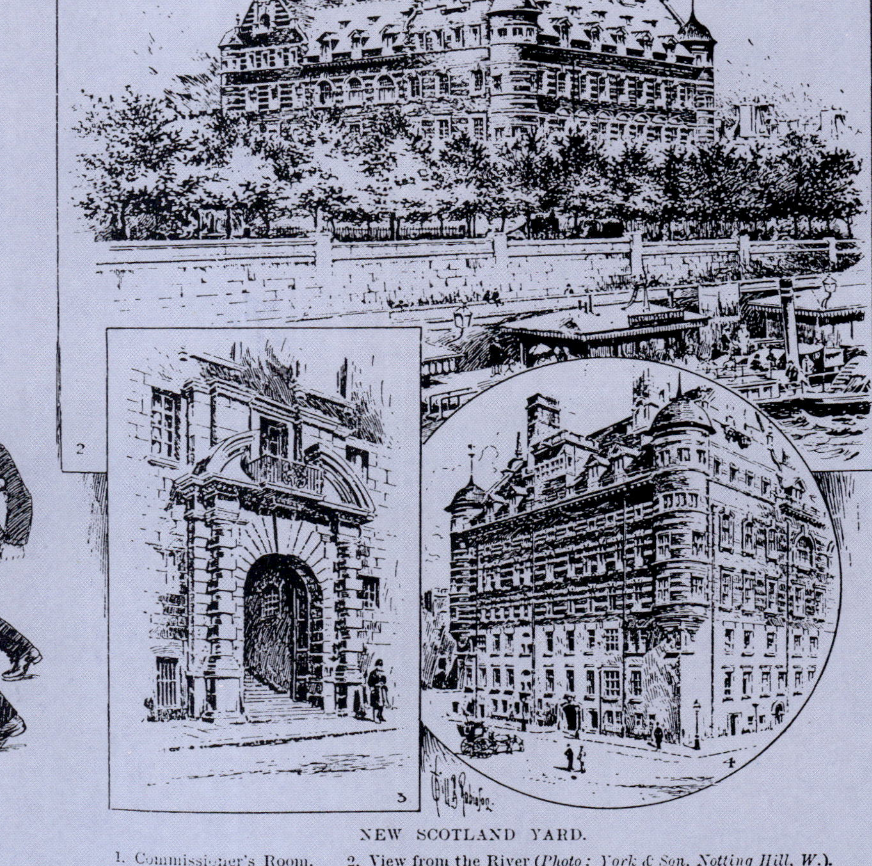

NEW SCOTLAND YARD.
1. Commissioner's Room. 2. View from the River (*Photo: York & Son, Notting Hill, W.*). 3. Principal Entrance. 4. The Western Façade.

Sherlock Holmes & THE POLICE

Watson didn't care for Lestrade. He was 'short, lean and ferret-like', and, in another story, a 'little sallow rat-faced' man. In *The Norwood Builder*, early on when he thinks he has solved the mystery, Lestrade is cheeky to Holmes; but as soon as he realises he has boobed, 'his overbearing manner had changed sudenly to that of a child asking questions of its teacher'. In *The Boscombe Valley Mystery* he begins by smarming up to Holmes when he thinks Holmes is on the scent, but when he thinks Holmes has gone wrong, he is 'indifferent and contemptuous'.

Lawson Wood. *End of play.*
This artist specialised in comic drawings of the police.

Lestrade went even further in *The Noble Bachelor*. According to Watson, he 'snarled' at Holmes and later 'shrieked' at him.

Extraordinary behaviour for a Scotland Yard inspector, but even this was not as bad as that of an Inspector Forbes in *The Naval Treaty*.

According to Watson, this 'small foxy man says 'tartly' on meeting Holmes: 'I've heard of your methods before now, Mr Holmes. You are ready enough to use all the information that the police can lay at your disposal, and then you try to finish the case yourself and bring discredit upon them'.

The impudence! Watson is too horrified to comment. Forbes soon gets his comeuppance, but even then the magnanimous Holmes gives him the chance of apprehending the villain and getting all the credit.

In the case of *The Second Stain*, Lestrade, played

'If there's a vacant place for a chief of police, I reckon you are the man for it'

by Colin Jeavons again, to save his face when once again baffled, makes out, as if by now anybody would believe him, that he is consulting Holmes only about 'a mere trifle' of a matter, 'nothing to do with the main fact...'

For the omniscient Holmes that 'mere trifle' is the clue to the answer to an altogether greater problem which 'that imbecile' Lestrade has completely missed, a problem, which if unsolved would have 'within a week', according to no less an authority than the Prime Minister, have involved Britain 'in a great war'.

Poor Lestrade. But as ever Holmes does not tell on him, but on the contrary lets him have his meed of praise.

In *The Sign of Four,* Athelney Jones of the Yard, played by Emrys James makes his first appearance. He is 'red-faced, burly and plethoric' and precipitate as well.

The Second Stain
Colin Jeavons as Inspector LESTRADE

Initially patronising – will they never learn? – the egregious Jones, records a shocked Watson, had the audacity to address Holmes in 'a sneering voice', but changed his tune as he got more and more out of his depth.

Baffled – they all got baffled sooner or later – Jones was no longer 'the brusque and masterful professor of common sense who had taken the case over so confidently'. No indeed. Now, 'his expression was downcast, and his bearing meek and apologetic'. He oils up to Watson and says, 'Your friend Mr Sherlock Holmes is a wonderful man, Sir'. But this time Holmes is not to be soft-soaped, and dismisses Jones as having only 'occasional glimmerings of reason'.

Inspector Bradstreet, whom we meet in *The Man with the Twisted Lip,* played by Denis Lill, was not a

'We're not jealous of you at Scotland Yard. No, sir, we are very proud of you, and if you come down tomorrow there's not a man, from the oldest inspector to the youngest constable, who wouldn't be glad to shake you by the hand'

The Norwood Builder
Colin Jeavons as Inspector LESTRADE

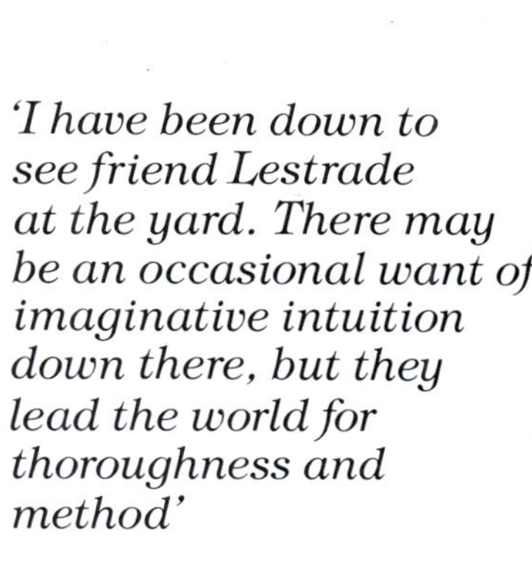

'I have been down to see friend Lestrade at the yard. There may be an occasional want of imaginative intuition down there, but they lead the world for thoroughness and method'

The Sign of Four
Emrys James as ATHELNEY JONES

The Man with the Twisted Lip
Denis Lill as Inspector BRADSTREET

Yard man, which may be why he and Holmes got on so well together. Bradstreet was in charge of Bow Street police station.

Bradstreet was always respectful: 'What can I do for you, Mr Holmes? I am sure, Mr Holmes, that we are very much indebted to you for having cleared the matter up. I wish I knew how you reach your results'. Bradstreet knew his place. Different from those show-offs up at the Yard.

The Abbey Grange
Paul Williamson as Inspector HOPKINS

The only detective Holmes really cared for was young Stanley Hopkins, played by Paul Williamson, seen here in *The Abbey Grange.* 'Excellent' Stanley would say when Holmes delivered himself of a deduction which Jones would have sneered at. 'I believe that you are a wizard, Mr Holmes'.

No wonder Watson in *The Golden Pince-Nez* refers with approval to 'young Stanley Hopkins, a promising detective, in whose career Holmes had several times shown a practical interest'.

In another story, *The Adventure of Black Peter,* Watson again refers with warmth to Hopkins: 'exceedingly alert, thirty years of age... a young police inspector for whose future Holmes had high hopes'.

This phrase of Watson's, 'practical interest': was there more to this relationship than might meet the eye? Had Holmes pulled strings to get Hopkins promoted? Could it be true, as suggested by one Holmesian expert, Mr Marion Prince, that young Stan was Holmes's son?

If so, did Watson know?

SHERLOCK HOLMES

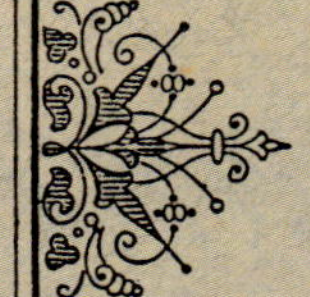

On Stage, Screen and Television

1901. William Gillette as Holmes in Sherlock Holmes at the Lyceum Theatre, London.

1922. Sherlock Holmes. John Barrymore as Holmes.

1929. The Return of Sherlock Holmes. Clive Brook as Holmes, H. Reeves-Smith as Watson.

1935. Triumph of Sherlock Holmes. Arthur Wontner as Holmes.

1939. Adventures of Sherlock Holmes. Basil Rathbone as Holmes, Nigel Bruce as Watson with Ida Lupino.

1959. The Hound of the Baskervilles.
Peter Cushing as Holmes,
André Morell as Watson.

1965. A Study in Terror.
Starring John Neville as Holmes and Donald Houston as Watson.

1973. Sherlock Holmes in New York.
Roger Moore as Holmes, John Huston as Moriarty.

1970. The Private Life of Sherlock Holmes.
Robert Stephens as Holmes, Christopher Lee as Mycroft and Colin Blakely as Watson.

Were the malignant Moriarty with a magic wand to erase Watson from the Sherlock Holmes saga, much of Holmes would be lost to us as well, since so much of what we know of him, the man and his deeds, comes from the pen of his admiring friend.
The immortal partnership has been presented on stage or screen more than a hundred times, some of its manifestations being illustrated here. Too often Watson has been portrayed as unintelligent, if not an ass, which misrepresents the relationship, and weakens the story. Watson is no slouch. He is a man of calibre, depth and mettle. When Michael Cox decided to make the Granada Television series one of his resolves was 'to get Watson right.' He has succeeded.

1978. Murder by Decree. Christopher Plummer as Holmes, James Mason as Watson.

Making the GRANADA SERIES

THE FLAGSHIP of the latest Sherlock Holmes series is *The Sign of Four,* the best of the four novels about Holmes, and in the opinion of most Holmesian experts the finest of the whole sixty-piece collection.

Certainly it has all the ingredients for a thrilling film: a beginning shrouded in mystery, a beautiful defenceless woman coming to consult Holmes about a strange request she has received; Holmes detecting and deducing at his dazzling best.

A visit in the dead of night to a strange house standing in a humdrum London suburb but out of this world inside, exotically furnished with oriental vases and tapestries, 'a carpet of amber and black so thick that the foot sank into it, as into a bed of moss', with 'two tiger skins thrown athwart it'; the owner a bizarre little man, smoking a bubbling hookah.

Now a tale within a tale, of violence, theft and bloodshed in the great fort of Agra in the Northwest of India. Then a mysterious murder in a weird setting; a face of horror at the window; grotesque and frightening figures.

Athelney Jones from Scotland Yard arrives to make his supercilious and sarcastic comments. Bungling things as usual, he arrests Mr Thaddeus Sholto, who is innocent, and would probably have arrested poor old Mrs Bernstone, the housekeeper, if Holmes had not straightened him out in time.

Soon, Toby, the tracking dog, 'with a most amazing power of scent' comes on to the scene. Then a whirlwind visit from the Baker Street Irregulars, a bunch of the dirtiest and raggedest little street arabs Watson ever clapped eyes on, Holmes's juvenile spies, who 'go everywhere and hear everything'.

The fast-moving succession of gripping scenes, each so different from the one before, accelerates to a climax in a breath-taking pursuit of the villains down the Thames in the dark – 'And there is the *Aurora,*' exclaimed Holmes, 'And going like the devil. Full speed ahead, engineer! Make after that launch with the yellow light. ...Heap it on, stokers! Make her do all she can! If we burn the boat we *must* have them!' Tantivy!

And have them they do. Justice is done. All is made clear. Everything is there in one story: crime, mystery, horror, suspense, the chase, and a happy ending. When Conan Doyle decided to pull out the stops, Hollywood had nothing on him.

For the same reason that it makes such a spectacular film, *The Sign of Four* presented problems in production. The greater the premium on drama and suspense, the greater the need for realism. Sequences which take place on ships at sea, for instance, if the action is restricted, can often be mocked up convincingly in the studio, like these two shots (1, 2) from the making of *The Abbey Grange,* showing Oliver Tobias and Anne Louise Lambert at the rail of a liner.

But when the action is fast and furious, camera crew and cast must produce practically the real thing. The steam boat chase on the Thames in *The Sign of Four* meant that they braved the real river in winter.

This sequence began and ended in mud, in a boat-builder's yard (3, 4), as Watson's narrative requires, the team using an inflatable rubber dinghy, which did not exist in Watson's time – though Conan Doyle foresaw their use as life-savers. Later, the team embarked for the chase. They were able to do this in more dignified style at Westminster steps (5). The crew set up their equipment in the stern of a modern support craft, Jeremy Brett, on behalf of Holmes, taking their salute (6, 7).

[1]

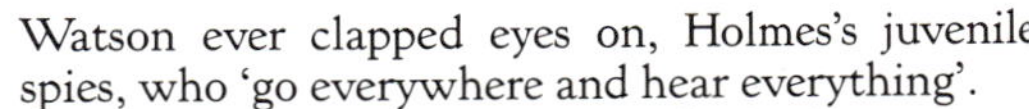

[2]

[4]

[3]

The two boats used (8) are authentic examples of the types in use on the Thames in 1889. The one used by the villains, 'the dainty *Aurora*', was a steam launch, 'as trim a little thing as any on the river...fresh painted, black with two red streaks...a

[5]

[6]

black funnel with a white band'. Holmes and Watson pursued her in a police launch, '...a very fast one...Holmes smiled with satisfaction as we overhauled a river steamer and left her behind us'.

If it had been visible, the modern London skyline would have destroyed the viewer's illusion of the Thames at night a hundred years ago, so the dinghy sets out (9), to blot it out by creating an artificial London fog.

The camera is in position. The Lighting Cameraman checks the light conditions (10, 11). Okay. Action.

Compared with the variety, complexity and technical demands of the fast-moving river chase

[7]

sequences, the requirements of other parts of *The Sign of Four* were less exacting.

Baker Street scenes were the easiest, for Granada built its own Baker Street, and though it stands not in London but in Manchester, in what was once a railway yard, Granada's Baker Street looks the same all the time.

As usual the day begins with a discussion of wardrobe (12).

Outside, below the first floor window from

[8]

[9]

which Jeremy Brett is here seen looking out, the director, Peter Hammond, briefs the Baker Street Irregulars (13). When, having received their payment for the day in advance, and, in Watson's words, they have 'gone streaming down the street', this is what Holmes would see looking down (14, 15).

The Sign of Four is so packed with different scenes that comparatively little of it could be shot in 'Baker Street'. Several elaborate sets had to be built

[10]

[11]

[12]

[13]

[14]

specially for this production, including the ornate home of Thaddeus Sholto, part of which is shown here (16).

There had to be a number of locations outside both London and Manchester, to which furniture, dresses and a variety of properties had to be delivered. Here is an Indian tiger arriving at his temporary home in Yorkshire (17).

Many scenes in *The Sign of Four* had to be shot at night. Filming in darkness requires a complicated lighting rig (18) as well as the usual camera equipment. The makeup has to be different (here's Holmes getting a final check-up, 19). It has to be done with the greatest care; nobody wants to interrupt the shooting to readjust it. It's approved. Holmes can now join Watson, and walk out into the night and the next action in the drama (20).

Many of the Sherlock Holmes stories are entirely or in part set in specifically described locations, which it would be pointless to try and construct for a single occasion – and very costly. Granada has made use of many settings outside London.

In *The Priory School*, for instance, for the stately home of the sixth Duke of Holdernesse, Holdernesse Hall, Granada was able to use Chatsworth House (21), one of the greatest houses in Britain, home of the Duke of Devonshire, a magnificent classical mansion built for the first Duke near Bakewell, Derbyshire, by William Talman between 1687 and 1707.

[18]

[19]

[20]

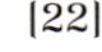

[22]

[15]

[21]

[16]

[17]

A splendid choice of location in more ways than one; many Holmesian experts agree that the sixth Duke of Holdernesse in *The Priory School* is modelled on the eighth Duke of Devonshire. The real and fictitious Dukes both have vast estates in the Peak District. 'Mackleton' in the story is Matlock in real life.

Of all the locations outside Baker Street the one best known to Holmes-lovers must be the spot where he was once thought to have fallen to his death in the grip of Professor Moriarty: the Reichenbach Falls in Switzerland. The two stunt men hired by Granada, Alf Joint as Moriarty and Marc Boyle as Holmes, show you how it happened (22).

'It is, indeed, a fearful place. The torrent, swollen by the melting snow, plunges into a tremendous abyss, from which the spray rolls up like the smoke from a burning house. The shaft into which the river hurls itself is an immense chasm, lined by glistening, coal-black rock, and narrowing into a creaming, boiling pit of incalculable depth, which brims over and shoots the stream onward over its jagged lip.'

Conan Doyle had seen the Reichenbach Falls earlier in the year on holiday with his wife, when he was already planning to kill Holmes off. A few months later he wrote to his mother: 'I am in the middle of the last Holmes story, after which the gentleman vanishes, never to return. I am weary of his name'. And, indeed, Holmes did vanish. But ten years later Conan Doyle brought him back, and *The Final Problem* turned out to be not the final problem after all.

THEME MUSIC

Original Music from the Series and the Film *The Sign of Four,* composed by Patrick Gowers, is available on T E R Records:
LP T E R 1136, Cassette ZC TER 1136 and CD TER 1136
Available in all good record stores or direct from
T E R Records at:
107, Kentish Town Rd, London, NW1 8PD

Send cheque or PO
for £5.99 for album or cassette
and £11.99 for C.D, post free,
to the above address

Allow 28 days for delivery